With thanks and love .... and
encouragement and to my girls: Zahra, Alysha, Nadia
and Tameera –wishing them all lifetimes of love.

Chapter One

The lobby had nearly emptied out in the fast darkening, early October evening. Five o'clock had come and gone. Most of the employees in the upscale office complex had scurried away from the old Distillery District to hop on a street car and head home.

Only two men remained. They were studying a document near where a security guard sat tucked away behind a half wall. The younger man, in his early thirties, slender in his hipster suit, looked up at his companion. Ten years his senior, this man was tall, solidly built and radiated power. His rugged features and jet black hair were set off by an impeccable grey suit. The younger man spoke at some length pointing to various sections of a document. The older man bent towards him nodding and responding.

The men paused briefly as a woman passed cell phone in hand. They heard her inquire of the security guard if a message had been left for her. At the negative response, she sighed gently, but audibly, and walked back towards the main entrance. She was simply and neatly dressed in a brown sweater and cords, her light brown hair plaited in a braid that hung midway down her back. Her full lower lip was held by her upper teeth.

The two men watched her push open the door, look up and down the street, and then disappear over the cobblestones towards downtown. "The girl from up north" said the younger. "Cole met her when he was up there doing the Wait Time project. They got the Emergency Room waits down to 45 minutes. I think it was her skills that did it. Cole suggested she apply for a position here, and promised God-knows-what. Her work is excellent, but I doubt we'll keep her long. She doesn't seem happy and when she gets an eye full of Cole and the new hire he's chatting up, I think she'll fly." The older man responded with casual kindness saying, "Likely homesick anyway, Jason."

"No, he mentioned she had no family left. More likely, she'll feel like a fool and run. Why do women fall for Cole? He knows she took him seriously, so now he's hiding out. Well, she's no teenager – probably 35 or so – and not much to look at either. Can't help there. Let's get back to this system plan."

Meanwhile, the woman had made her way north on Trinity, across to King, and up Sherbourne. She walked quickly across to Queen Street, dashed nervously up a flight of dank stairs, and entered her small bachelor's apartment above Johnny's Grill. The bass line of the jukebox kept her awake each night till 2 am, but it was all she could afford in the city and it was just a 15 minute walk to work.

Now, sitting on the daybed that doubled as a sofa, with her shoes and coat still on, and her purse clasped in her hands, she gave way to tears. She admitted to herself that she had left her friends, the town she knew, and the beauty of the north for a mirage. She had spent her meagre savings to relocate for a man who had been full of empty promises and full of himself. She had been the worst kind of fool.

Sitting there, in the dejected light of one uncovered bulb, she went over the past seven months and every word Cole had said. He had never actually promised the future she had built up, her head in a cloud of rosy daydreams, but he had certainly led her on, toyed with her, and just as certainly tired of her now.

And what an idiot she had been – alone after losing old Mrs. Ginsberg, who had fostered her after her parents had been killed in a car accident when she was ten. She had been so lonely again and it had looked like Cole would change that.

For the six months he had been in North Bay, he had singled her out, flirted with her at work, partnered with her on projects, and taken her out. He'd mocked the size of the town and joked that they would get to every single place to eat in town before he left. He had shown no interest in visiting her foster sister or in the First Nations community that was such a big part of the area, but she had excused that due to his being so career-oriented.

Towards the end, he had suggested she really show off her work skills on his big project and then apply to head office in Toronto. Hadn't he meant that he wanted her to be with him? He had told her she was gorgeous and while she had known it to be untrue, how could she resist? "Dear Lord!" she hung her head in her hands. She had done half his work for him! Had he not really expected her to come to Toronto? Looking back over the past month, she realized that Cole had not been too eager to make time for her, but she had believed his claims of big projects and tight deadlines.

In fact, Cole had already been bored with her when she had shown up to surprise him with the news that she had been hired to manage terminology for a clinical systems project in the province's capital. She was now working in his very division at the health informatics consulting firm that took up the entire second floor of the old Victorian building close to the shores of Lake Ontario.

Cole had thought it was a great joke that she had followed him and had shared the story of her infatuation with half the office within a week of her arrival. Her colleagues all liked her and felt sorry for her. It had been immediately apparent that her sweet inexperience had been no match for Cole's skilled womanizing.

Now, a month later, he had tired of even bothering with her. It was no longer amusing to lead her on with careless kisses and claims of being busy or off-site. The desperate girl was still texting him to meet up! Jenna struggled to hold onto her dreams, making excuses for him. She had felt his impatience and sneering. But dreams die hard and she had told him she needed to meet with him one last time. Cole texted back asking her to wait in the sushi place next to the office at 5 pm.

Jenna had sat alone at the table for two for 45 minutes, slowly admitting to herself that he was not going to arrive. She had sat drinking the whole pot of green tea in the pretty little ceramic cup exploring a new possibility for Cole's behaviour every time she poured. Maybe he had left a message rather than texting? Maybe he had had to rush out and left his phone on his desk?

The tiny doubts she'd been ignoring had come crashing in. She had known there would be no message but had returned to work to ask anyway. Finally, back in her small apartment, she sat on her bed trying to think what to do. She wanted to leave immediately, to pack her bags, go to Union Station, and hop on the train back home. But she no longer had a home. Mrs. Ginsberg's grandson's lawyer had sent a brief letter asking her to vacate within two months, take her bedroom furniture if she needed it, any linens she wanted, and to choose something to remember Mrs. Ginsberg by. She'd selected a plate from Europe with a field of sunflowers. It had reminded Mrs. G. of home. "You just can't find a real field of sunflowers here." She had said, "And never the right oil for sauerkraut." The plate hung now on the wall in Toronto but Jenna knew it wouldn't stay there.

Jenna still felt she needed to see Cole one last time. Perhaps he had misunderstood something she'd said. After all hadn't they imagined where they'd holiday, where they would live? Why, he had even said any kids they had would have blue eyes for sure.

She got up, washed her face, and looked at herself in the mirror. She looked the same as always, pleasant but unexciting. Everything about her was uniform at first glance: eyes - plain blue, hair- plain brown, skin - plain white. She examined the sad downturn of her generous lips. Mrs. Ginsberg would have pierced her with her sharp gaze and said, "Dearie, there are those who never got to feel heartache."

Jenna squared her shoulders. She took off her work clothes, hung them neatly, and washed her bra, her underwear, and her socks in the sink. She hung them to dry on a coat hanger on the shower curtain rod. She would get her first pay cheque on Friday. She had planned on searching out some decent second-hand furniture and a TV but now she had no idea what to do. Maybe if she had a new haircut and a new outfit she could rekindle what she and Cole had had? The women and men in Toronto were more smartly dressed than she had ever been. She shook herself.

She made some toast with jam, ate a piece of cheese, brushed her teeth, and lay down in bed, prey to a night of restless images and snatched moments of sleep.

The next day during the morning break, Jenna sat with two colleagues for coffee. They had heard the rumours and wondered if they should've warned her about Cole. She was such a nice person and she didn't deserve this. Jenna Martin was a stranger in the city and they worried about her. She was paler and sadder than she had been and a bit less plump. They had no idea how to help her since she was such a private person so they just invited her to join them again at lunch.

Back at her desk in the shared office, Jenna immersed herself in the data they had collected on clinical decision-making. Thinking through what doctors versus nurses versus support workers needed to know to help a patient kept her from having time to think about Cole but suddenly she couldn't bear not seeing him. What were the words of that Alysha Brilla song? "Love is such a rush. Heartaches are its bookends." She thought her heart was breaking for him now. She remembered how at the start she had also ached for the sight of him.

She quickly thought of an excuse to go into the area where he worked with the systems team.

Cole saw her entering and sensing a possible scene, leapt from his desk, grabbed her arm, and hustled her into the large document room. "Buttercup, my apologies. An emergency came up last night." She stared at him, not smiling, not nodding, not affirming him as she had ridiculously done for half a year. She bit her lip as she fought the desire to hope. How sweet it would be to hear him beg forgiveness so that she could indeed forgive him and reclaim the plans she had had for her life.

A silence stretched out and then she said, "You lied to me, you deceived me, you messed up my life." "Listen", he replied with a sneer, "There's no law against dating. If you read more into it than that then you're an idiot. Anyway we're finished. No harm done. Show some gratitude. You loved it and now you have a good job far away from that godforsaken wilderness. Bye darling."

Suddenly a huge and righteous anger boiled up inside her, "Don't ever call me darling again!" she snarled her voice rising. Cole laughed. "Oh for God's sake, act your age! You've been around the block a few times. You'd think we had planned to get married and have kids." She flinched and then flinched again when he laughed and said, "My God. Did you think I would spend the rest of my life with you? You're not in my league darling. You must have been out of your mind."

Jenna said then in a quiet and sad voice, "Yes, I was. Please. Go away." He left without a glance, leaving her standing there watched by the older man who had been in the lobby the night before. He reached behind and opened and shut the door so it seemed he had just entered via the second door by the photocopier.

Jenna looked over surreptitiously, wiping tears from her cheeks. Turning quickly she walked to the door she and Cole had left by. But as she reached to open it, the stranger arrived silently behind her. He placed his hand on the door, handed her a tissue, and said "Jenna Martin, right? You joined the company recently but we haven't met. I imagine you're feeling homesick. I was just going out for some lunch. Why not come with me? Turn around. No need to hide your tears. They make us human, you know."

He had a gentle yet compelling voice. He spoke with the authority of someone used to having orders followed and so she turned around tilting her chin up. He was a half a head taller. She had not seen him before. She would have remembered him. He was tall, ruggedly handsome, well dressed, with dark hair just starting to grey at the temples.

"Do you work here?" she inquired. "I do indeed," he smiled kindly and held out a large, warm hand - engulfing hers and patting it with his other hand. "Étienne Beaulieu. I'll meet you at the entrance in five minutes. Grab a sweater. It's chilly and we'll walk."

He was waiting for her when she came off the elevator wrapped in her old, brown, hooded shawl. His overcoat looked expensive and she wondered who he was. She worried that she was too shabby beside him but he said easily, "There you are," and held the door for her as they went out into the weak October sun.

It was damp and chilly and Toronto looked its worse. The bright leaves of the maple trees in autumn had recently fallen and their sad brown remnants blew about the street.

Étienne took her elbow and hustled her across the busy intersection, down a trendy side street, and into the main part of the Distillery District where trendy restaurants beckoned on every side. He steered her into a cosy French-Canadian restaurant and chose a small table in a warm, back corner. He laid her shawl on an extra chair. When he removed his coat, she saw that he wore a beautifully tailored suit, an immaculate white shirt, and a silk tie with a gold pin.

He smiled easily at the approaching waiter and suggested to Jenna that they should perhaps start right away, "Maybe some soup - their French onion? And perhaps Montréal Corned Beef sandwiches to follow?" She agreed and chose fries as a side. He placed the order and poured some of the tea he had requested as they were seated, keeping up a steady flow of chitchat so that she could not start to cry again.

The tea was as comforting and warm as his hand had been when he had introduced himself. Under the gentle influence of his casual questions she began talking, telling him more than she realized, more than she had yet acknowledged about herself. He refilled her tea and asked what had brought her so far from home. A wave of misery swept over her as she realized how homeless she was. She wished she could tell this kind man how foolish she had been with Cole but she didn't even know who he was.

His phone vibrated continuously in his pocket but his focus remained on Jenna. He felt a kinship with her heartache having travelled the same sad route and he was loath to leave until he was sure she would be okay.

"And your parents?" He asked so softly she hardly realized she was responding to a question when she replied. "My parents both passed away after a car accident when I was 10. I was raised by a wonderful foster mother. She passed away this spring. She waited for the lilacs to bloom and then slipped away. She loved lilacs."

His hands, warm and strong, covered hers and then he kissed the back of the top hand in a silent salute to her loss and she registered that he must be French though his English had only the faintest accent. His kiss was the first warm, prolonged touch of support she had been given in a long time and she felt her breath steady and slowly deepen in response.

Jenna realized they had been silent for a while when he said, "Come, mon chou. Let's walk a bit and then head back to work. Have you seen Little Trinity Anglican Church? It is the oldest church in Toronto- built by the poor so they didn't have to pay pew prices at St. James Cathedral. The cost of the cathedral was partly paid by the early settlers paying a subscription. Come, let's walk. It's a lovely old church. You'll see lots of lilacs there come spring."

They walked out into the damp cold and he kept up a steady flow of history. The brisk pace brought a glow to her cheeks and a shine to her fine eyes with their fringe of short thick lashes. He pointed out aspects of the church and town as they walked and then asked if she planned to stay in the city.

"Well, I have a six month contract," she replied and suddenly a wave of longing for Cole wrapped around her. Images of the Cole she had dreamt up left her quiet and miserable once more. Just for a few minutes this kind, gentle man had steadied her but she felt tears threatening anew and spent a moment pretending to examine a historical plaque.

"You're miserable and if you ever need to talk, let me know," he said with a smile. "Why are you so kind to me?" she queried, looking up into his dark eyes. "Didn't someone say that to participate is to be truly human?" he asked, "I feel you would do the same for me or anyone." He smiled gently. They were back at the lobby. She smiled back at him, "Yes, I'll pay this forward. Thank you so much Mr. Beaulieu."

"Call me Étienne, please. Back to work with you and stay away from the document room. It seemed to have a bad effect on you." He watched her enter the elevator, then briskly turned around, and strode to the parking lot where he got into a Mercedes S550, and drove away. He had meetings out of town for the next three weeks and his busy mind soon forgot Jenna.

Jenna had dreaded being back at work but the task of sorting through numbers and information soothed her and it was soon 5 o'clock. She stopped at a small grocery store and selected a carrot, a parsnip, a celery heart, and two potatoes. Once home, she set her only pot on the burner, chopped the onion into the melting butter and steadily added the vegetables in fine, small, evenly matched pieces to the pot. Mrs. G. had always said, "Worries go down better with soup than without."

Quieted by the familiar actions, she relaxed, added water, brought the soup to a boil and then turned it down to a steady simmer for half an hour, tossing in some of the chopped dill she'd frozen, and salt and pepper at the end. She sat down slowly stirring in a spoonful of sour cream. Every time Cole's image entered her mind, she superimposed it with that of her kind champion from lunch. "Look to the light," her foster mother had always said. She should've seen Cole for the slime-ball he'd been. She knew Mrs. G. would have.

Jenna hadn't expected to sleep but within minutes of tucking her blankets tightly around herself, she fell into an easy slumber but on waking, she was weighed down once again by the realization that she had uprooted herself for nothing, and at the age of 35 was all alone in Toronto. She knew this grief would pass but in that gray October morning she could not see how or when. That jerk, Cole, was not worth another thought. She had been lucky to have wasted only half a year on him. She would move back north and focus on her career. Yet the thought of her career just depressed her. Everyone else seemed to have so much more than work.

She arrived at the office before nine, her usual quiet and steady self, responding peacefully to queries in her musical voice, and ignoring the irritability of her manager. The day finally ended and she stopped at a second-hand store to buy a book and left with five. Maybe they would bring some life back into her. The fifth one was free anyway and books were her solace. They were also her only evening companions.

Jenna had never had a big income. Her dreams of going away to college were set aside when her foster mom, by then in her early eighties, had fallen ill and was no longer self-sufficient. How could that have been 17 years ago?

Jenna had started working at a medical office near home, learning various aspects of health information management and getting her diploma and certification. She'd always managed to make ends meet but she'd had to learn to buy clothes that would last. If she had always envied people who could shop without major calculations and compromises no one knew, for she wasn't one to complain. "Complaining won't buy the baby booties." as Mrs. G had always said.

Now, as autumn approached winter, she took to wandering the Lakeshore for hours after work, breathing in the cold air like a punishment. The huge ocean-like lake held steady at her left as she walked towards Harbor Square Park. Her eyes sought out bits of green and beauty - mementos of the North. She'd stand looking blindly out at the island and then start walking into the city.

She'd stop only when she found a little restaurant that looked like it had a nice soup and she'd eat it, savouring every drop. The wait-staff never minded the small order for she was kind and gently friendly. The 30 extra pounds she had carried for years started to melt away as the weeks passed. Then four or five more pounds too many came off so that her clothes hung from her frame, the pants now belted, and her eyes became almost too beautiful in her pale, gaunt face.

Cole was always around at work, haunting her thoughts, though he never looked for her or even at her. Yet three weeks later, her eyes still sought his presence. "Lovesick, stupid puppy" she said loudly to herself as she rounded the corner and ran smack into the large, reassuring chest of Mr. Beaulieu. He steadied her with his hands, gentle but firm on her upper arms and she looked up. Her fine eyes were caught in a shaft of light so that the darker circle around the blue and the golden brown around the iris glowed brightly. He noticed how the lack of makeup let him just enjoy the colors. But why was she still pining? And was that a belt or a rope hiking up her pants?

"Steady on" he said and smiled. She smiled back, her full lips curving upwards and turning her plain features into something warmly magical. It was so nice to see him again. He steadied her on her feet and looked as if he was about to chat when he was hailed by a group heading into the main boardroom and with an apologetic glance and smile left her to join them.

"Now, there's a man," she thought to herself, and somehow that evening as she left work she found herself window-shopping, examining the pretty clothes in the windows of the trendy shops that surrounded their office. She did need something new for the office – something that actually fit and flattered her. It was a good thing the stores were already closed she thought, as she caught sight of a few price tags. There was nothing here she could afford anyway but she would need a winter coat soon. November would be upon them next week. Clothes, and not Cole, absorbed her thinking for the first time in a long time and she headed for her Lakeshore walk with a lighter step.

The following day, Étienne sat down at the desk of his trusted assistant. "What do you know of Jenna Martin?" he asked. Reassured by the praise he heard and the quality of the report that Jenna had written on the impact of big data needs on the day-to-day work of healthcare coders, he asked if Mrs. Bond thought Jenna would be a good complement to his presentation in Montréal in two days. "Would the heath information management people find her an asset?"

Mrs. Bond, happy at last to find a way to help Jenna, said that absolutely, she would be well received. "Good then. Could you check if she's able to travel on such short notice? Tell her to prep 3 to 5 slides and 10 minutes on her current project and arrange her flight with mine for tomorrow? Book her a room for the two nights. Oh, and also, book a table at Beaver Hall for six for the first night. And get her address, please. Tell her I'll pick her up at 7 am tomorrow."

Mrs. Bond nodded efficiently then pursed her lips and said, "She may not have anything decent to wear." She could see that her boss was setting his impressive mind to work by his downward stare and fierce expression. He soon looked up and laughed saying, "Not to worry." as he headed back into his corner office.

Mrs. Bond set off to discuss the conference opportunity with Jenna and the idea was received with surprise and excitement. Jenna threw herself into preparation. She had always felt that she had something to share but had never submitted a proposal to a conference. Now, she would be part of a workshop with Mr. Beaulieu.

It was clear that Mrs. Bond was very fond of her boss. Jenna had googled his name and was astounded to discover that he was the owner of the company. She would've found it daunting to present with him if she didn't already know what a dear man he was.

The thought of leaving the town where Cole was, even for three days, felt like it would be a taste of freedom. Jenna was ready to move on.

Chapter Two

The next morning, Jenna left her apartment just before 7 and stood outside watching people come and go at the mental health centre across the road. She was chatting with a homeless man when the Mercedes slid to a quiet stop in front of her.

Mr. Beaulieu was in the passenger seat and a man she'd seen at the office was driving. Mr. Beaulieu hopped out, took her suitcase, popped it in the trunk, gave five dollars to the man she had been chatting to, and got into the back seat with Jenna.

After introducing her to Jason, he asked her if she had her ID with her in her purse. She said that she did and the three of them chatted gently as Jason drove them the 5 kilometres to the Billy Bishop Island airport. Jason would have the car for the three days and was quite chipper about having his own wheels for change, though he supported the use of public transit above cars and mocked the fact that it took them 45 minutes that morning to transverse a small corner of the city by car.

When they pulled up in front of the ferry terminal, Mr. Beaulieu asked her to grab a luggage cart while he explained something to Jason. When she returned, she was horrified to see that Jason had driven off and her suitcase was not with the bag at the curb. "Oh no", she said, "He's gone off with my bag! Can you call him?"

Mr. Beaulieu, turning away to hide the pleased look on his face, replied, "Unfortunately, too late. We'll just be able to board in time. I'll call the cab company and have your bag held. The company will purchase outfits and other essentials for the conference. Let's move quickly and get aboard!" She accepted this. In fact, Jenna was immediately rather excited about the idea of getting new clothes. His little ploy had worked out smoothly.

Once in the airport and through to their gate, they were left with 15 minutes to spare. Jenna asked her boss to explain the plan for the workshop and he did, saying that her focus on the changing work requirements at the coding level would balance his explanations of where healthcare data was going and that she could have up to 25 minutes if she wished. She could wait and see how it went and decide how much time to take.

Once on board and in the air for the short flight, Mr. Beaulieu apologized and pulled out his Blackberry. Jenna tried to hide her excitement, looking out the window, and at the hostess. "Is this your first flight, mon chou?" he asked turning to her with the beautiful smile that brought laugh lines to the sides of his mouth and eyes. She replied, "I never had the chance to fly before."

Jenna gave him a big smile that lit up her face like a Christmas tree. He looked away thoughtfully as she turned back to the window, wondering how he had ever thought her plain, and then resumed answering emails.

The hostess came by with an offer of beverages and Jenna listened enviously to Étienne's flawless French. Of course, like most Canadians, she had studied French all through school but she struggled with all but basic expressions. She was relieved when the hostess automatically switched to English for her.

Jenna had heard the Quebecois could recognize the Anglais just by body movements and fashion sense - or perhaps, rather, a lack of fashion sense she thought ruefully. She was suddenly very glad that she would not be wearing her own loose-fitting clothes at the conference. If the company didn't provide enough money, she would put in some of her own. She was saving her money to head back to North Bay so she had a paycheck in her bank account. Spending some money on clothes wasn't a bad idea.

In Montréal, they collected the one bag and then went to hail a taxi. It took them to the Intercontinental Montreal across from the Palais de Congress where the conference would start the next morning. They checked in and went up in the elevator. It was Jenna's first hotel. Their rooms were situated next to each other.

Étienne suggested they meet again in an hour in the lobby to shop and then have lunch. He would be busy with a meeting in the afternoon but would make some suggestions for her introduction to Montréal.

She had had trouble using her card to open the door and he leaned over her, directing her hand. She responded within seconds to the feel and smell of him. My goodness, he was yummy. She gave herself a shake to bring herself back to reality as she said thanks. He was probably married with 5 kids, though she'd noted he wore no ring. Anyway, if she was out of Cole's league then she was way out of Étienne's. However, she was quite happy being his cabbage, 'mon chou', if nothing else.

She walked into her room, across the soft carpet, and straight to the window. There across the river was the oddest yet most attractive architecture. She recalled it was the Expo 1967 housing complex designed by a famous architect. She craned her neck to see all of the sites along the St. Lawrence. A flock of birds took flight and she smiled. She would grant herself some freedom to enjoy.

She examined her room. It had a huge bed, desk, coffee and tea station, and a glorious tub in the bathroom. She felt like soaking in that tub right away. How she had missed having a tub! The shower in the apartment was a sorry substitute and she was always cold in that place. She stripped off her clothes, folded them on the end of the bed, and hopped into a lovely bubble bath. She soaked in water just nicely on the hot side, watched the water as it drained, rinsed off, dried with a huge, Turkish cotton towel, and dressed again. This was the life, she thought as she sipped herbal tea and watched the boats. I've been missing out!

At 11:45, she was down in the lobby, admiring the restaurant where they would have their Quebec specialty buffet breakfast the next morning. She knew she should gain a few pounds back and anyway she had always loved food. Mrs. G. had taught her to chew slowly and savour every bite. She needed to slow down and enjoy again.

Mr. Beaulieu got off the elevator and she was struck at how handsome and elegant he was and how real his charm seemed compared to Cole's. How had she been so taken in? Étienne's girlfriend, if he had one, was one lucky lady.

They took a 5-minute taxi ride to Boulevard Saint-Laurent and he told her about some of the buildings as they passed. It was cool but sunny. Soon he ushered Jenna into a large boutique. Bold as brass, he walked up to the three fashionably dressed women at the counter and said, "My wife has lost her suitcase. We need two outfits suitable for a conference, something pretty for the evening, something warm to go over top, and underclothes for three days." He then switched to French, handed over his credit card, told Jenna to have fun, and, with a lingering kiss on each cheek, said he would fetch her in an hour for lunch.

The ladies look quite animated and happy with the task he had set. One ushered her to the dressing room area, set her on a sofa, and then asked her for her favourite colours, and whether she preferred silky or cosy fabrics. She soon switched places with another sales clerk who measured Jenna's feet and asked her to step inside the huge change room and strip to her undies. Another then knocked, came in, and measured every part of Jenna, and told her to wait. One of them was soon back with a number of the most beautiful bras and underwear sets possible. She showed Jenna how to lift up each breast as she bent forward so that it fell back into the cup and

Jenna looked up in amazement at the change the bra made to her shape without being at all uncomfortable. She was whipped in and out of 7 or 8 bras and asked to choose three she liked. They told her not to worry when she said she expected to gain a bit of weight back– the bras were fitted to allow for some mild weight changes. She chose a white, black, and beige, but insisted she would just get whichever one went best under the clothes she bought.

The saleswoman smiled knowingly and as she left, added the pale rose to the pile of three. She also added matching underwear and camisoles to the collection. Jenna was asked to leave the black bra on and to put on the camisole that matched it. Somehow her own clothes had been whisked away. If Jenna had known anything about clothes, she would've known that the four underwear sets, alone, cost far more than two weeks of her salary.

Skirts and blouses were brought in and she was asked to choose those that caught her eye. She was worried that the colours were too bright as she generally wore shades of brown but she loved the cherry red blouse and the navy silk skirt and the navy blouse with its matching swirling skirt. The casual elegance suited her. She looked lovely and well cared for in the expensive cuts. For the cherry blouse, they brought out a gorgeous pashmina shawl in navy with the same cherry running through it and a gorgeous button up cashmere sweater for the navy outfit. They set stockings on the pile and then brought in the dresses.

She fell in love with one of the dresses at once. It was like something from the 1950s and when she settled it over her still generous hips it was comfortable yet flattering - exposing far more breast than she was used to - but maybe that was just the bra? Her breasts had seemed so much smaller since she had lost weight but they seemed almost to be begging for attention in this outfit.

The saleswoman handed her a beautiful hooded cape in artisan wool woven in different shades of blue and hazel with a little gold - exactly like her eye colour. She felt like a princess in it as she twirled around. Shoes came next and then a casual sweater and jeans and a long-sleeved t-shirt to go under the sweater. Somehow in 55 minutes she was standing at the front of the boutique with 10 bags at her feet and Étienne was collecting her, signing the receipt, waving off her protestations of thanks, and telling her she looked wonderful in the navy sweater and jeans with the cape over top. "I'm starving." he said, "Lunch is right across the street at Le P'tit Plateau." He had the bags delivered straight to the hotel with instructions to have them put in her room.

The restaurant was lovely and they chatted easily. They started with superb, tiny servings of fish soup, foie gras au torchon, and a smoked salmon plate, followed by Jenna's first cassoulet -tender lamb on a bed of beans. Étienne enjoyed the enthusiasm with which she ate each item. Thirty plus years had not taken away her childlike ability to enjoy yummy food, and Étienne found that his food tasted all the better for being with her while she ate. By the time they finished off with coffee and shared a crème brûlée and chocolate mousse cake on a crunchy praline base, they had solidified a comfy, easy friendship. "We're like a pair of old slippers, mon chou." He said and she smiled. Somehow it felt like the best of compliments.

He said he had arranged a special Calèche tour around the town after lunch. It would be a one hour horse-drawn carriage ride and then she could wander back to her room. He had reservations for one of his favourite spots in Montréal for 7 pm where they would meet some old friends and she must make sure she was hungry again by then.

The horse and driver were waiting outside and he handed her up onto the seat. "Don't worry about being cold." he said. "The seat is heated and there is a warm blanket right here. I have paid and included the tip so just enjoy. He'll let you down a street away from the hotel at the cathedral. Amuse-toi bien." He kissed her on both cheeks and was off in a taxi. Jenna was glad that there was a map with all of the main points explained and numbered because the driver, although he kept up a voluble explanation as they went, was very difficult for her to understand at the beginning. By the end of the tour, she had become accustomed to the way he pronounced English and was enjoying every minute of his humorous explanations. The 17th-century French settlement had an interesting history.

Back in her room, Jenna unpacked and hung her new clothes, feeling as if it was Christmas day back in the years before her parents had died when she had been their beloved Jenny. Years of not quite belonging had wearied her but how fresh she had felt just now walking into the lobby in her lovely clothes with her Montreal tour providing new images and knowledge.

She undressed and lay down, luxuriating in the crisp white sheets and expensive duvet. Before she knew it, there was a knocking on the door and it was dark outside. Grabbing the housecoat and throwing it on she dashed to the door and said, "Who is it?" opening the door on Étienne's reply. "Dearest" he said pulling the lapel of the housecoat over her left breast, "You look very inviting but can you possibly meet me downstairs in ten minutes?" With a quick apology and violent blush, she shut the door, brushed her teeth and threw on her new outfit, careful not to snag the stockings. She left her room, brushing her long hair, as she ran down to the elevator.

Étienne was sitting in the reception area, relaxed, and looking like he had not been busy at all that day. She noticed his eyes sweep her legs and the shining curtain of her long hair and she realized why women loved wearing high heels and dreamt of being Rapunzel as kids. It was interesting this modern tension between being comfortable and equal but also wanting to revel in femininity. She expertly twirled her hair up in a bun and secured it with a pin knowing he was watching.

Jenna had worried needlessly about dining with his friends from university days at McGill. They created a friendly, welcoming atmosphere bouncing between English and French but always updating her and keeping her a part of the conversation. She learned that Étienne's father had been a Quebec mining magnet who was retired and was now widely respected for his work on First Nation's land rights. It was clear Étienne admired his father's courage and convictions.

After a delicious meal in which Jenna enjoyed her first ever tortière, they bid au revoir and she and Étienne walked back to the hotel, parting ways in the hallway with just a pleasant good night and arrangements to meet after the morning plenary in the room where they would present. Jenna felt reluctant to see him go but slept almost as soon as her head touched the pillow. It was hard to welcome sleep when reality was better than any dream.

The next morning's presentation went amazingly well with Jenna's section generating quite a few questions and commendations. Having worked for years in the complex world of medical coding, she understood the concerns and needs of her colleagues even better than Étienne and she knew that his congratulations to her at the end on her successful presentation and his pride in her were genuine.

Étienne was busy that evening so Jenna joined a group on a dinner theatre trip and then read a book in the bath. When she lay down, her mind was buzzing with what for her, with her quiet lifestyle, had been two days of real adventure. She thought rest would elude her but by 11:30 she was deep in a sound sleep. The next morning they met in the lobby for breakfast chatting amiably about the conference as they ate their crepes and other goodies, enjoyed coffee, and then caught a taxi to the airport.

"Are you happy with us?" He asked. "Yes, very." she replied, "It's good to do meaningful work." Settled in their seats she heard him give a sigh of pleasure and say, "You're such a restful companion." Her ears yearned for "mon chou" but she supposed even the French were not always liberal with their endearments. They arrived back in Toronto to find the car waiting and soon they were back in the office each busy with their own work.

The rest of the week and the next passed without Jenna catching even a glimpse of Mr. Beaulieu. He had been in the office just briefly catching up on work with Mrs. Bond who had been pleased at success of the Montréal trip and his positive comments about Jenna. Étienne's ears perked up when Mrs. Bond mentioned Jenna. He had hoped to see her but had been so busy that the tension was getting to him. He rubbed his neck and said, "I'm 42 now. Am I foolish to be thinking about a new relationship?" "No sir", said Mrs. Bond, "Probably just approaching the age of reason." They smiled at each other. Mrs. Bond had been married 30 years and was a firm believer in the peaceful love and consistency. She had actively disapproved of Étienne's first wife. Mrs. Bond had never met a person so much more interested in money and attention than commitment. "I guess I'll see Jenna next week at the all employee meeting," he said as he went to his office. Mrs. Bond sighed happily imagining a big church wedding.

He was in fact to meet Jenna that very night. He'd worked late and she had dined with her workgroup at Archeo's. It was a new restaurant and they had gone to try the pizza and pastas and congratulate each other on the successful launch of a web portal for primary care physicians and their patients. The company had sponsored the celebration which added to the festive air. Jenna had felt she was a valued part of the team. Now she walked humming along to the traditional carol. They had already started Christmas festivities in the square though it was still November.

Jenna strolled along enjoying the sight of the annual Christmas market. Soon she had passed into the industrial no man's land that separated the Distillery District from the bridge across the expressway to the lake. She saw Étienne off to the right leaving their office building and thought of yelling hello but over 200 meters separated them so she walked on.

Suddenly, she heard growling to her left between the rows of shipping containers and the piercing cry of a dog being hurt. She yelled "Étienne! Étienne!" loudly and waved frantically at him. As soon as he caught sight of her and started running she dashed between the rows of containers to be brought up short by the glare of two tense coyotes who seemed to be planning to eat a mop for dinner. No, not a mop she realized but an unkempt poodle mix cowering away.

Étienne was behind her in a minute, grabbing up a piece of cardboard and swinging it and yelling loudly at the wild creatures. When they saw her also advancing with her purse held high, they disappeared into the dark without a sound. "Wow, so scary." she said and he agreed adding somewhat harshly, "Never approach a pack of coyotes like that. They can kill you." "I know", she said, "but look at this poor little lamb." They both squatted down trying to approach the quavering dog but it backed away. "I'm going to grab it or it will be lost in the dark and it might be injured." He asked her to block the left and sat down in his designer suit with one leg stretched out covering the right and before she knew what was happening he'd reached out, grabbed the nipping dog and pulled it into his chest directing its mouth away by grasping its head firmly much like she done with grass snakes as a child.

For long seconds the dog struggled and then suddenly stopped, seemed to listen to Étienne's calm, praising voice and then subsided with a tail wag against him. My goodness, she thought, he could even charm dogs.

"Okay", he said, "reach out a balled fist and talk quietly. I can feel that he's calm and feels safe now. Poor guy." Indeed, when she spoke gently and held her closed hand to the dog's nose, he licked her. "There's blood on his leg," she said. "Let's get him to a vet." Étienne rose up with the dog tucked against his formerly light gray camel hair coat. "There's a vet at Sherbourne and Richmond." she said. "I pass it every day and the sign says it's a 24-hour emergency centre." They started walking as that would be quicker than getting his car and taxies only accepted service animals.

"It looks like a stray. I've never seen a stray in Toronto before." Jenna said. "Only up North and then only big dogs." "Strange, eh?" he replied. "But from the bones I feel under all this matted fur, I'd say he hasn't known a good home for a while. Maybe a backyard breeder tossed him out."

They entered the warmth of the vet's office and the receptionist came to them exclaiming over the dog. She asked if they could provide a credit card to guarantee payment, entered it, and quickly ushered them into an examination room. "Just keep holding him till the vet comes and we can put him on the table when we need to." Étienne and Jenna stood close together stroking the dog whose tail thumped more and more often. "Do you think it's a poodle with a long tail?" Jenna asked. "He has to be mostly poodle to have fur that keeps growing but he has such long legs and such a long snout."

The vet entered and listened to their adventure while gently examining the dog. "He's underweight and lacking vitamins but I see no signs of fleas." she said. "The puncture wounds are superficial but he'll need a rabies shot. Let's get him on the table." She took the dog's vitals, checked thoroughly, told them it was a girl, administered several injections and deworming, and concluded by saying, "You saved her life. She was defenceless out there eating garbage and prey to coyotes. Do you want me to call the Humane Society to pick her up? She has no microchip. I doubt that she is anyone's pet." "No", they both said simultaneously, "We'll keep her." The vet smiled with relief. "Well, she's a lucky girl. You seem like a lovely couple."

Jenna was a little anxious at the cost of the vet bill but Étienne told her not to worry. He added in the recommended vitamins, food, shampoo, dog collar, leash, bed, blanket, and suggested that Jenna grab 5 to 6 toys. Never having been able to shop without checking prices and totals, she enjoyed adding in a winter doggy coat in Hudson's Bay colours and sturdy food and water bowls. The receptionist suggested a full clip the next day but showed them scissors that they could use to at least make the dog more comfortable as they gave it a bath.

Étienne paused outside the door. "Now, where to? My car?" "No." said Jenna, "My apartment is two blocks away. Let's go there." They walked briskly up towards Queen. She saw flash of disbelief and concern cross his face as she opened the unlocked street door and led him up the smelly stairs to her door. Inside, he said "You live here?" with a scornful look around and she bristled up informing him that not everyone could afford a hoity-toity penthouse. She didn't notice the chagrined smile that crossed his lips.

Étienne unpacked the supplies on the counter since there was no table. He admired the pretty plate on the wall and the flowers suspiciously like the ones from the office boardroom. She saw his glance and smiled. "I rescue the flowers from the garbage most nights and rearrange them here."

"Ms. Martin, you are very resourceful." he replied. "Let's get this little lady into the bath. Oh, you have no bath. OK then – the kitchen sink. Can I borrow some track pants? She is livening up. How about calling her Zoe? It means "life"."

Zoe was not keen on getting washed but soon settled into the few inches of warm water allowing them to cut off masses of hair so they could get the shampoo near her body. He noticed the apartment was spotlessly clean and had cosy touches despite the size and lack of furnishings. The place was so small that he could see the bed with its beautiful quilt, embroidered cushions, and hand-knitted throw from where he stood by the sink. Despite the cramped area, he was reminded of his aunt's farmhouse in rural Quebec.

After several removals of wads of hair, replacements of water, and rinsings of shampoo, they realized they had a cream-colored, midsize poodle – terrier mix with the cutest brown eyes. "I can take her." said Étienne. "No!" said Jenna sharply before he could explain the dog would alleviate his loneliness, "I need her." "Then let's both have her, but she lives here with you," said Étienne. She heard a sad resignation in his voice and hastened to assure him he could be with them whenever he wanted and that it was just that she was so lonely in the city.

She had been rubbing the damp dog as dry as she could and now she handed Zoe over to Étienne. She saw his eyes linger on her breasts. "Sorry," she said. "My first wet T-shirt contest." And Jenna blushed when he looked again quite deliberately and said she would have won hands down.

She didn't have enough towels to get the dog dry so they used her t-shirts too and then sat together on her bed. Zoe, wrapped in one of Jenna's sweaters, slept on Étienne's knee. Étienne was looking hilarious but quite unfazed in her baggiest tracksuit, his long legs only half covered. They had given Zoe her small meal and would feed her four times a day as she adapted to having full nutrition again.

"Now I'm starving," said Étienne, and Jenna made an omelette and homemade fries, and heated two bowls of the soup she had made the evening before. Holding a relaxed Zoe he watched her manage in the small kitchen and felt soothed. He imagined her cooking up a feast in a kitchen that had counter space to spare. Dinner ready, he transferred a dry and exhausted Zoe to the bed and they ate happily chatting about the rescue, past pets, Montreal, and work. Their plates rested on an upturned cardboard box with a linen tea towel over it. He ate with relish, thanked her, and kissed both her and the dog on their noses.

Étienne had called a taxi and watched for it from her window "It's not safe for you here." he said wishing he could just lie down with her and keep her safe. "I'm fine," she retorted.

"Don't walk the dog in the dark," he added but she didn't answer. Obviously, once Zoe was dry and rested she would need to go to the washroom again. Étienne left, checking that the door was locked.

Jenna tidied up, humming happily. How good it felt to help a fellow creature! How quickly doing an act of kindness made one's own troubles lessen. Zoe woke up and Jenna checked that the dog was fully dry, then grabbed a bag, put on the dog's collar, coat and leash and, dressed warmly herself, she took the little dog across the road to relieve itself. Jenna lifted her nose to the wind sensing the approach of snow from the north. Back home, they slept within minutes, Jenna's hand resting on the little dog curled up by her knees. It was so good not to be alone.

Chapter Three

Jenna enjoyed taking the dog out and feeding her. All her life, she'd had opportunities to care for others and life in Toronto had felt empty without that. She sat with Zoe on her knee, carefully clipping off more fur and wondering if she should make an appointment with a groomer or wait to talk to Étienne. They had exchanged cell phone numbers for Montréal but she hesitated to call. At 9 am, a text came in. "Can I drop by and bring breakfast? Then we can take Zoe to the groomer." She replied, "Yes, please," and swept and dusted the apartment. Jumping into the shower, she quickly dressed and smiled at her bright eyes and glowing skin in the mirror.

Étienne arrived 30 minutes later with coffee, bagels, cream cheese, and a cold cut and pickle tray from Caplansky's deli. They enjoyed the food and the sight of the little dog, looking less lean already, waiting hopefully for a scrap. They agreed to never feed her until after they'd eaten, but to always save a piece.

Jenna, usually on the quiet side, was amazed at how easily she chatted away, her lips curved into a continuous smile broken only when she shared how she had lost her dog when she had been taken into foster care and had never found out what had happened to him.

Étienne held her hand and said worrying over a loved one was one of the worst pains in life. He listened patiently as she described the big, goofy dog who had been her childhood companion. He told her of his own early childhood and all the scrapes he had gotten into. She laughed at his comic re-enactments and exclaimed over his many scars. She longed to run her fingers down the one on his chest and hoped he had not noticed the way she had instinctively licked her lip.

The day was wonderful. It was not yet the busy season at the dog salon and the groomer took extra care after hearing about their little rescue. Though Zoe emerged looking thinner and almost hairless, she pranced about, very proud to be clean, light, and feeling pretty. Under all that hair there'd been a sweetheart of a dog, not classically good-looking, but with a whimsical appeal. They both agreed they had never thought of having a small dog but that life taught you that you didn't always know what was best.

They returned to Jenna's place mid-afternoon and ordered authentic Chinese from an upscale organic restaurant. Jenna had protested against ordering the meal for four but Étienne had reminded her how great Chinese leftovers tasted. They lay on the single bed together watching two old comedies and laughing like teenagers. Jenna was sad when he closed his laptop, took the dog out, and then said good night with the hug and kiss of a good friend.

She knew that she would remember this as one of the best weekends of her life. She had a new companion in Zoe and had solidified her friendship with Étienne.

Monday morning Étienne went straight to his trusted assistant's desk, "Mrs. Banks, can we still arrange for Jenna to accompany me to the international conference in Argentina? And is there any chance you could watch our small dog?" Once he heard back that a seat could be arranged and Mrs. Bank loved the idea of a pet for a short time, he emailed Jenna.

Jenna was hard at work analyzing a coding problem when the new message icon popped up on her computer screen. She frowned. She opened the email and was relieved to see that it was a message from Étienne. She had had an email from Cole earlier that morning asking if she felt like having a little of what she was missing at a hotel that night. Jenna had felt ashamed and humiliated and had replied firmly stating that if he ever contacted her again, she would file a harassment complaint with human resources. But now here was Étienne and she felt the promise of his kindness washing away Cole's ugly behavior.

He wanted her to go to Buenos Aires for five days! She had two weeks to get a passport. Jenna opened the application online. A rush order might just work. She emailed back and Étienne said they'd risk it and book her flight. He told her to expand her presentation from Montréal to include an international perspective and to talk about the project they done for coding refund submissions for Canadians who had been treated while traveling abroad. For a moment, self-doubt assailed Jenna. Perhaps she should wait till she knew more? And then she heard Mrs. G.'s voice saying,"Just hoping and waiting makes many a person a fool." It was true. She would go abroad.

Jenna reviewed her wardrobe. She checked and found that the weather would be 28 to 36°. She would need a summer outfit and a sweater in case of air-conditioning. She alternately worked on her actual project, her presentation, and her travel plans. The day that had started with the pain of Cole's email had become one of opportunity. You just never knew. She'd be having a sunny break from the dry cold of November in Toronto.

Jenna's passport arrived within seven days and she packed and repacked her one suitcase. She found a pretty dress in a rack of summer clothes at the back of a trendy boutique. It had been 70% off so for next to nothing she had a gorgeous linen shift and matching jacket. The shade of dark blue was charming on her and the saleslady found a raspberry red scarf to add some color.

The night before their flight Jenna had her presentation saved on a stick, printed out, and emailed. Zoe had settled happily in at Mrs. Bank's apartment. Jenna was all set. That night she thought she would be too excited to sleep but within minutes of laying her head on the pillow she was resting peacefully.

The next morning, Jenna stood waiting by the curb feeling a sense of adventure she had not known for decades. Once again Jason dropped them off but this time out in Mississauga at the big international airport. Jenna smiled at Étienne and he smiled back. For some reason she blushed and turned to look out the window. Étienne was surprised. He hadn't seen a woman blushing in years. Jenna was an old-fashioned person in many ways. He admired how she'd wound her long hair up on her head like a princess from long ago.

Once on the plane they were led to first-class seats. Jenna's eyes widened in surprise. Étienne shrugged, "It's a thirteen hour flight. Even with the plane change in Chile, it's a long-haul. We need to be comfortable."

They were delayed taking off and Jenna realized that she needed to check her period. "Is it okay to use the washroom now while we are waiting?" Étienne nodded yes. Jenna's period was heavy as it was the first day and she sighed as she sat back down. She was looking pale. She pulled the pins out of her long hair and leaned back with it spread like a silky curtain all around her.

The plane took off smoothly. Étienne ordered some juice for them and said they needed to keep hydrated. He tucked a blanket around her knees. Jenna contemplated how kind he was and she felt tears prick her eyes. "What's this?" he asked and then he grinned. "I have two sisters. Is it that time of the month?" Jenna nodded. Étienne kissed her gently on her forehead and said, "Here, put your chair back. Let's wrap you in two more blankets, heat your seat, take these two Tylenol, put on this night-shade, have one more kiss, and rest for an hour."

Surprisingly, Jenna fell into such a sound sleep that they were well over the Caribbean before she awoke to the sounds of lunch being brought around. "Hungry?" asked Étienne his smile crinkling up his eyes. "Flying always makes me ravenous. Look what we have - apricot chicken, a rice medley, and some kind of salad. Looks pretty good." And all through the next 5 hours, he cosseted her. She thanked him as they prepared to watch a movie and he said, "I think we were destined to be great friends." Jenna gave him her beautiful smile but at the back of her brain niggled the thought that she would never be satisfied with only that.

The airport of Buenos Aires was quite near the city core and Jenna felt a surge of excitement as they circled to land. Neither of them had been to Argentina and both were eagerly looking out the window. Jenna held her breath when Étienne leaned in to look at the view with her. It was so tempting to just snuggle her face into his neck. She wondered how anyone could smell so good. His deep voice stopped her musings, "No use in rushing to get out as we have to wait for the baggage. Shall we just sit for a few minutes when we land?"

They sat making sightseeing plans and then walked leisurely along the route to the baggage carousel. Jenna reflected on how nice it was to have someone planning everything out so smoothly. Cole had never done anything for her. She realized now that one should not give and give without reciprocity. She could hear Mrs. G. muttering, "If you'd been twice as smart with that Cole, you'd still have been an idiot."

As they approached the long, scary-looking escalator Étienne gestured to Jenna that a woman was struggling to manage her kids and stroller and carry-on bags. Jenna could see Étienne was hesitating to approach as the Mom was in full hijab. Jenna asked if they could help and the woman smiled in relief. Étienne took the stroller and bags and Jenna and the woman each carried a child. The woman turned to them when they reached the top, "Such a huge escalator. I was worried. Thanks so much."

Jenna recalled a day at the mall with her friend Nisha and Mrs. Ginsberg. The two girls had been mocking some Somali ladies whose long, colorful dresses and turbans seemed out-of-place to their young eyes. Suddenly Mrs. G had grabbed them both and pulled them to the wall. "Never look at another human being with contempt," she hissed angrily two spots of colour high on her cheeks. Then she dropped her hands and unheard of tears glistened in her aged eyes. Cupping Nisha's brown cheek in her pale, blue-veined hand she said, "Hate is the easy road my 'Bubbala.' Never take it." Jenna could still recall the moment that tough little Nisha had turned her head to kiss the palm of Mrs. G's hand and then raised her chin and said, "I promise."

Jenna looked at Étienne calming collecting their bags and a strangers and she took in the swirling humanity around them. Airports and travelling were places for lessons as well as fun. She vowed to be a gentle traveller.

Étienne pulled each bag off the carousel as it came around. Their new acquaintance said, "I'm moving here to join my husband so we have a lot of luggage. It's such a struggle to travel alone. You are both so kind. Do you two have kids?" Jenna shook her head and the woman smiled widely and promised to pray for them to have a child soon.

When the woman had left with a porter, Jenna turned apologetically to Étienne and said, "So sorry. She thought we were married and I didn't bother to explain." Étienne laughed and said with a wink, "I would not mind adding a little physical effort to her prayers." Jenna smacked his arm. They grinned at each other.

They got a reputable-looking taxi and Étienne asked the driver in quite fluent Spanish to show them 2 to 3 sites as they headed to their hotel, the Hub Porteño, in the cultural centre of the capital. The driver said it was a 20 kilometer drive till they reached the section of the city called Recoleta and then he would show them the plaza, the famous cemetery, the library, and the tango cabarets.

Never having been outside Canada, Jenna was astounded at the heat and the noise and the energy and the beauty of the city. Étienne translated the rather colorful history of Buenos Aires the taxi driver shared. She could tell he spoke fluent Spanish. Étienne tipped the driver generously as they got out and the driver gave them his card telling them to watch out for fraudsters and to call only him.

The hotel was gorgeous. After they checked in, Étienne left Jenna at her door telling her not to worry if she slept till morning. She ran around her room. Her eyes drank in the beauty. The understated elegance of the room, the extravagance of the bathroom, and the delightful view from her wrought-iron balcony made her clap her hands. She could see the old mansions and then the sandy beach and blue waters of the Rio de la Plata spread before her right outside her balcony. She wished she was seeing it all with Étienne beside her so she could share impressions. Jenna sighed and admonished herself, "You are getting too attached to him, my girl."

Jenna took a quick shower and climbed under the cool sheets. She was lay awake imagining various scenarios for the next day all of them involving Étienne suddenly developing an irrevocable passion for her. She slept through dinner and woke the next morning feeling refreshed and eager to start the day. The sounds of this city were so different from Toronto. She couldn't wait to explore. She got up stretching and stood on the balcony grateful and expectant.

There was a note under her door from Étienne asking her to meet him for breakfast at 9. She showered happily, blew her hair dry, left it hanging free down her back, and dressed in jeans, a pretty blouse, and sandals made her way to the lobby.

On the way down in the elevator, Jenna had read a sign promising free tango lessons each day at 4 PM. Étienne greeted her with his usual Quebecois double kiss but also ran his hand down the length of her hair tugging on the ends. She told Étienne about the tango lessons as they got settled at their table. The waitress greeted them with deliciously strong coffee and buttery croissants which they enjoyed while waiting for their fruit and eggs. "I would love to tango," said Étienne. "What do you think? Am I too old and too big for it?" Jenna frowned at him, "You are in your prime. The two of us are just approaching the age of reason and you would be an awesome tango dancer. Let's see if the lessons fit our schedule. I brought the conference brochure." Jenna paused as Étienne pulled his chair around so they could pour over the 3 day "at-a-glance" listing of events. Today was theirs and each day the conference finished at 3 and then commenced again with an optional but enticing evening event.

Today they would stroll the Recoleta visiting Eva Peron's tomb, the art gallery, and a museum. After lunch out somewhere nice, they would review the presentation and then take their first tango classes at 4!

At the cemetery, they lost themselves among the flowering shrubs and gorgeous family mausoleums trying to decipher the Spanish inscriptions and imagining the wealth and histories of the community. Then they headed arm in arm to Nuestra Señora del Pilar Basílica where they admired the architecture and lit candles for their loved ones. Jenna was getting hungry when they arrived at the Recoleta Cultural Center but forgot all about lunch when she stood before the exhibition of Xul Solar's paintings. Étienne watched her face as she traced her own emotions in his multi-layered, whimsical yet weighty works. She stood for a long time before some of the most complex of his paintings and Étienne slipped away to buy her a set of prints all Xul's works in beautiful colour.

They passed a boutique selling hats and scarves and he insisted on buying her a pretty straw confection. "You are getting pink from the sun." he insisted, "I won't have you faint on my watch." She thanked him prettily with a hug and asked why he didn't need a hat. "My Metis blood," he smiled, "I never burn." Great, now she was picturing how their children might look with her fairness and his dark, good looks fighting it out genetically. Hadn't someone said that we are homesick most for that place we have never known?

Étienne presented the prints to her at lunch and she blushed furiously and said, "You shouldn't have. You didn't need to get me this." To which he responded, "Not everyone appreciates Xul's search for universal harmony mixed with political commentary. His paintings spoke to you. I wanted to get you this souvenir, ma cherie. Accept sil vous plait." He folded a kiss into her hand and she quietly said thank you with tears shimmering in her eyes. Étienne cleared his throat and sat back contemplating the terrace overlooking the courtyard gardens. He knew it was too soon to tell her of his fledgling feelings.

If Jenna had known the cost of a meal at Duhau Restaurante, she would have worried but unfamiliar with haute cuisine and Argentina's money, she happily perused the menu. The waiter suggested that they start with a visit to the cheese room where they selected a small plate of artisanal, regional cheeses. As they savored the cheeses with a special marmalade and local bread, they settled on sharing the 'seleccion de mar para dos persona'. Étienne had enjoyed many a fine meal but had never enjoyed anything more than the unselfconscious pleasure with which Jenna fed him tidbits and enjoyed the cheeses herself. "I'll gain back every ounce I lost," she exclaimed to which Étienne replied, "And if you do? You'll still be healthy and they'll be even more of you to admire. We each have our own shape and shouldn't worry beyond health." Étienne stared at Jenna from under lowered brows wondering how he had failed to notice before how her eyes sparkled when she was happy and how she pressed her hand to her heart when she spoke. One day he would get her a necklace to sit right where her hand so often rested.

When their platter arrived, they could not believe the beautiful presentation of seafood, rice, potatoes, and vegetables. By the time they had eaten their lemon sorbet, enjoyed their coffee, discussed each print by Xul and reviewed their presentation plan, it was time to walk back and get ready for their first tango lesson.

They moved slowly. Étienne told her how travel and jet lag could change the perception of time and space. "In a wonderful way," Jenna exclaimed. "I feel like I will look back on these few days as a glimpse of forever."

They met at the door of the tango room. Jenna, a bit overwhelmed by the heat and the bright sun, had showered and changed into a pretty dress. Étienne looked distinguished in a crisp white shirt and dress pants his hair still wet. There were four friendly German couples there as well and the tango masters soon had them performing the basic steps, a simple "ocho", and some of the core movements.

As soon as the wonderful music had begun, Jenna had lost her shyness. She was surprisingly light on her feet and agile as she spun around the room in Étienne's arms. They loved the tango and when the hour passed, Étienne offered the teachers a tip with a request for 2 more songs for them to practice. The private instructions were just what they needed to find the right balance. The tango masters complimented them and said that they simply must get tango shoes before the next lesson and suggested the best tango show for them to attend that night.

She met Étienne that evening feeling a bit underdressed for a tango show but he told her that she looked very pretty so she got happily into the taxi. How wonderful it was to be looked after for a change! Being independent and always worrying was not all it was cut out to be. The driver dropped them at El Querandi where they enjoyed consommé, Ensalada Griega, a pasta called Ñoquis de Rúcula, and shared a Semifreddo de Limón for dessert.

"You must have found my soup and omelette pretty primitive," Jenna commented. Étienne smiled, shook his head, and said something in French. "What did you say? Jenna asked tilting her head in what he considered an adorable way. "Just that "C'est le ton qui fait la chanson. It is the tone that makes the song." Étienne replied turning her arm so that he could kiss the sensitive inside of her wrist. They walked back hand-in-hand listening to the sounds of Buenes Aires. Étienne stood outside her door, said an abrupt goodnight and then turned, saw her looking at him expectantly and began kissing her passionately. Her hands went to his neck she found herself pressing her eager body against his. Within seconds the heat between them was at a peak and when she felt his lips nibbling from her ear to her breast, she moaned. A few seconds more and there would be no stopping. He said, "Wait, Jenna. Not yet." and they pulled apart staring at each other with parted lips. Jenna said she had better get some sleep. Étienne kissed her palm, watched her safely into her room, and left. She lay in bed reliving each moment again and again.

The next day, the room was full for their presentation and it was clear that Étienne was a powerful force in the informatics world. When he stood to speak, the room quieted immediately and she felt a surge of pride at the way he effortlessly impressed the audience with his ideas. When he held out his hand to introduce her, she trembled with nerves and he kept hold of her till she steadied and then slipped to his chair. She felt that she could not follow his brilliance but her ideas were equally useful and soon the audience was nodding and taking notes and she was on a roll. As they got into the taxi that afternoon, he kissed her with enthusiasm and then leaned back laughing and saying she had stolen the show from him. Her whole body hummed with excitement. Life was amazing suddenly and she was looking forward to another tango lesson in his arms and then a different tango show with the conference group.

Étienne directed their regular driver to the premier store for tango shoes and they were fitted and then feted as they tried on a variety of beautifully tooled shoes. "You never get coffee and Piononos in a Canadian shoe store," exclaimed Jenna happily as she sipped the dark brew and munched a pastry. Étienne kissed a bit of strawberry and Chantilly cream from the corner of her mouth. She swallowed at the sheer sensuality of his movements.

"How much will the shoes cost?" Jenna stammered while blushing. "Can you manage $50?" Étienne asked knowing that offering to pay for the shoes might make Jenna feel shy. "Oh, yes," said Jenna "They are all so beautiful! Feel this leather." Jenna could not bear to take off her chosen high heels and sat turning her ankle this way and that. Étienne grabbed her foot unstrapping the shoe tenderly and teasing her saying, "These shoes are too sexy for daylight. I can hardly think looking at your feet in them. Let's get them in their box and only bring them out when we're ready to … dance." Jenna laughed delightedly at his deliberately lustful expression and teased him about a shoe fetish.

Of Argentina, Jenna's best memories would always be the dancing and the tango music. Together they learned the complicated steps. Jenna relaxed in Étienne's lead and they dipped and swirled in perfect harmony.

On the flight home they studied the tango books they had bought and planned to find a tango club in Toronto and meet weekly. Jenna gazed at Étienne's greying temples and laugh lines as he slept. Whatever happened, his friendship had been a gift and she would treasure it.

Chapter Four

Zoe was glad to see them when they stopped to pick her up and Mrs. Banks had clearly enjoyed having her. They had forgotten how small and energetic she was as they attempted to gather up her many bags and scoop her up. Laughing they said their thanks and farewells to Mrs. Banks whose usually serious face softened as she saw how natural they were together. She even winked at Étienne as Jenna puzzled over her cryptic comment about Zoe being good practice for them.

Soon Jenna was cuddled up with Zoe on the sofa in her apartment going over the photos on her phone and reliving the wonder of their trip. She set her alarm extra early so that she could walk Zoe and do something with her hair and face. She knew she was hoping to attract Étienne. There was no harm in trying and anyway as Mrs. G. had always said, "Lightning strikes more trees than blades of grass." Being a bit more noticeable might not be a bad thing she thought as she straightened her Montreal skirt.

Each morning Jenna walked with Zoe till her cheeks glowed and then showered, brushed her hair till it shone, left it hanging down her back, and applied a light lip gloss and mascara. It was a pity that her efforts were wasted as there was no sign of Étienne. He waved at her a few times as he rushed from meeting to meeting with a work team at his side but he had cancelled both times that he had promised to come to see Zoe and have dinner. He finally showed up unannounced and fell asleep as she prepared some eggs for a light dinner. Jenna tucked a blanket around him and kissed his brow. He slept the night waking to her gentle kitchen noises as she tried again with some new eggs. They ate, walked Zoe, and were just starting to research Tango lessons on the net, when he got a call and rushed off to an early meeting. As he left, he said something about them having the next day and then was gone.

Jenna had woken the next day with a happy feeling of anticipation, but he texted saying something rather urgent had come up, so she and Zoe enjoyed the snowy day together. It was the Saturday before Christmas, but Jenna had no shopping to do. She had already prepared a gift for her dear foster sister, who now lived on the Nipissing First Nation's Reserve about 45 kilometers from North Bay. Nisha had come to Mrs. Ginsberg the same year as Jenna and they had been best friends ever since. Jenna had invited Nisha to spend Christmas with her in Toronto, but Nisha was heavily involved with youth programming for the community over the holidays so had promised to visit at Easter. Jenna had wrapped and sent a sweater she'd knitted. She would wait until Christmas morning to open Nisha's gift to her. It sat, beautifully wrapped, under a pine bough. She'd seen Étienne reading the tag the morning before. Jenna decided to go grocery shopping and cook a nice chili and homemade buns for Sunday in case Étienne came by but there was no word from him.

Monday morning, Jenna left Zoe with a promise to run home for lunch and headed off to the office. She had four days of work and then she would spend her 10 day holiday with the dog. Étienne was a caring employer and only essential staff worked the end of the year. Everyone else was off with pay from Christmas Eve till the day after New Year's and those who worked got time and a half. It was no wonder the employees were so loyal.

It was freezing out now and Jenna's nose was running when she arrived at work, so she went straight to the women's washroom where she pondered the kicking feet of a small child sticking out from under one of the cubicles. The child was saying "Stupid. Stupid. Stupid. Stupid." as he lay on the washroom floor. Her nose blown and her hands washed and dried, Jenna squatted down, and took a look under the door. "Lucky we keep this place so clean," she said to the little blonde chap while assessing him.

Ten years in a busy foster home had given her a lot of experience with kids. This fellow was around three, very upset, and it would not be easy to settle him. She squatted down. She told him the story of the dog rescue in her lilting voice adding in all the details that she knew would interest him, and making the coyote incident as dramatic as she could. By the time the villains had skulked away, the child was quiet. During the revelation of the pretty dog underneath all piles of fur at the groomers, the child had inched out and was lying beside her. She told him she'd finish the story as they washed their hands which they did several times, watching the bubbles drift away in the gentle stream of warm water she had set. Jenna then asked him if he'd prefer to walk or be carried. He opted for carried and she took him out, figuring he must belong to one of her colleagues.

Down the hall, Mrs. Bond was looking worriedly around. She was trailed by a petulant looking beauty in her early 30s. "Thank God. Thank you, Jenna." said Mrs. Bond. "Here he is." Étienne was walking calmly towards them, his eyes registering the child held snugly in Jenna's arms. "Jenna", he said, "You've met my son Philippe. Come on buddy." He took the child gently from Jenna and headed back to his office followed by the elegantly dressed woman.

Jenna had feared he might be married, but he could have said so. Didn't he know how quickly a person could imagine the future even when they forbid themselves? She went to her desk, sunk down in regret for something she had never even articulated to herself, shutting her mind to all but her work, reminding herself that Zoe would be waiting by the door when she turned her key.

Three hours later she looked up to find Étienne at her desk. "Can you join me for lunch?" He asked and hesitated as he noticed the shutter that had come down over her eyes. He still hoped for the best. "Twenty minutes to eat and then we can see to Zoe?"

Over big bowls of soothing udon soup with tempura, he asked if he could talk to her seriously. She said, "Of course." He told her that he had been married, it had not worked out, his ex-wife had taken their three-month-old son and left him. She had granted him few visits but ensured he paid full support for her lifestyle. He had done so willingly, but missed not knowing his son. Clarisse had called him yesterday to say she was re-marrying a man younger than herself, who had no patience with kids, and anyway, she had found she was not cut out for motherhood. She had brought Philippe to him that morning and had just left.

"I need your help. I need you more at home than I do at the office." he said and then paused and ate some soup. The nerve, she thought, asking her to leave a professional job to babysit. But already her heart was wavering. They needed her – first, the dog, and now, the child, - two little lambs that needed love.

"I'd wanted to spend more time with you first," he went on, "but we are both past our youth and have been burnt by romance. I think we would get on very well and Philippe and Zoe would have a happy home. I feel peaceful when I am with you. Will you marry me, Jenna? We can grow old together." He saw the shocked look on her face and went on, "You can take some time to decide, but I see no reason why we shouldn't be compatible. You understand my work and what it means to me. We get along so peacefully together. You're calm and kind. It would be best for Philippe to have a permanent mother. His own has often ignored him and has just all but abandoned him." Jenna sat staring at him, an adorable crease between her eyes. He wanted to smooth it away with a kiss but didn't want to rush her. "Don't respond now," he said. "I know it's sudden. I had not expected this turn of events. You would not suffer financially. I know this sounds like a business proposal, but neither of us is sentimental." He kissed her hand, finished his soup, settled the bill, and drove her to her apartment, where they took Zoe for a quick walk.

Back at the office, he told her to think about it, and walked off as calm as could be while her mind was seething with conflicting feelings. She sat at her desk. Where was the love she'd always dreamed of coming with marriage? Here was her first ever proposal and it was pretty flat. She reviewed every word that he had said. She had sounded like a passive dairy cow – calm, kind, and peaceful. He had suggested she was too old to expect romance and too sensible to wait for a knight in shining armor. He had said they wouldn't be intimate until she wanted to and she could just let him know. How embarrassing! Her cheeks flamed again as they had under his quizzical look. As if she would one day go up to him and say "Hey, let's get jiggy."

An hour later, Mrs. Bond came by with Philippe and asked if Jenna could keep an eye on him while she made a few calls. Jenna said, "Of course." She hadn't been able to focus on work at all anyway. She drew little pictures and told Philippe the story of Zoe again adding in even more details and titling each picture. She held him on her knee and soon he fell asleep, his head heavy and warm against her chest, and his little hand resting against her stomach. She kissed his blonde hair and closed her own eyes. It was always so nice to hold a sleeping little one. How she had dreamt of having a child one day and now one was being offered to her.

When she opened her eyes, rested and more peaceful, Étienne was settling into the chair by her desk. "I won't press you about marriage now, but could you help me get him settled in my apartment tonight and to shop for what he needs?" Jenna knew he needed someone to look after his son, but he needed to step up too. "Yes," she said, "We can pick up Zoe and get you organized together." "Great", he said and gently lifted Philippe up. "I have made a little bed for him on the sofa in my office for now." She missed the warm weight of the sleeping child. Étienne was not in love with her, but maybe they could love the child together. Two of her colleagues stopped by and she left her whirling thoughts behind as they reviewed a work plan.

Five o'clock came quickly and there was Étienne with Philippe holding his hand. She shut down her computer, got her purse, bundled up, and walked out with them.

Étienne was now carrying a car seat that he had picked up at Canadian Tire. He wrestled with installing it while the car warmed up and Jenna and Philippe made snowballs. Once driving, he asked her whether it was better if they all shopped together or just one of them got some basics. It had turned out that Philippe had just one suitcase of clothes with him. Jenna felt a pang. She'd seen many children come into foster care with only a bag of belongings. "Let shop together, she said, "And then pick up Zoe."

The GPS took them to a big kid's store and she suggested the boys take a cart and get toys while she picked out clothes. She loved shopping for kids" things and picked out 10 outfits, underwear, PJs, and a snowsuit. Philippe had a nice winter jacket already. She remembered mitts and got three sets with matching hats and scarves. She rounded a corner to find Étienne laughing loudly as Philippe sat in a police car pretending to arrest him. They had a cart full of cars and trucks and Lego and had clearly had a good time. Étienne hugged Jenna. "Look", he said. "I thought I'd never get a chance to be a dad for him." His eyes welled up with tears. "I hope Clarisse is happy and we can be happy too." Jenna realized it must have been so hard for him to not be with his son and to be worrying about him constantly. She hugged him back and said they had better get the dog.

Étienne pulled up in front of her place, asked her to bring stuff for a few nights, and all the dog things. She ran up, no longer feeling worried. Her decision didn't have to be made now. Nisha had often shared with her the wisdom of a First Nation's chief, "So long as mists envelop you, be still; be still until the sunlight pours through and dispels the mists as it surely will. Then act with courage." Jenna would wait.

They drove to Étienne's apartment off Queen's Quay, parked underground, and he suggested they take Philippe and Zoe up first, then, he'd come back for the rest of the things. They got into the beautifully done elevator and were whisked up to the penthouse. "I apologize," he said, with a smile "I recall you're not overly fond of hoity-toity." She saw with relief that he was laughing. Inside, she looked around. It was a beautiful condominium apartment, but not the ideal place for a little boy and dog. It was splendid though with its view of Lake Ontario and the gorgeous kitchen she could see to her left.

"I'll take the dog out, then get the first load, and then keep putting stuff in the foyer here. Look around. Every window is child-proof. Make yourself at home, and maybe see what we can do to make Philippe's room work. The spare room is beside his. Welcome." he said and kissed her fully on the lips for the first time.

Jenna took off their outer things and hung them in the large hall closet. She paused, touching Étienne's freshly laundered camel hair coat and remembered that night, so recent when they had rescued Zoe, that now seemed part of her life before. Before what exactly, she pondered.

"Where's your room, sweetie?" she asked Philippe but he said he didn't know. "Wow", she thought "Poor guy. This is all new to him. Soon he'll be crying for his mom." They had best make sure he had a calm evening. Mrs. G."s first priorities had been to make sure a new child was fed, watered, and put down for a rest. Mrs. G. had encouraged Jenna to stay on for free after her public support ended at age 18 and she had helped Mrs. G. with an ongoing succession of children in need of sanctuary.

Jenna turned down the hall and opened the first door on the right. It was all set up with beautiful furniture but it was designed as a nursery. They'd have to let the crib side down so Philippe didn't feel too much like an infant. "Okay buddy", she said, "Here's your room." "I'm not a baby", he said and threw himself to the floor setting up for good scream. "Of course not", said Jenna "We're saving your baby furniture in case a new baby comes. We are going to get you a big boy bed tomorrow. Do you want it shaped like a car? Is it ok if Zoe has her bed right here? Where should we put your new toys? Oh, I hear daddy. You take Zoe and I will help with the bags."

The little dog seemed to understand Philippe's anxiety and circled his ankles forcing his hugs and pats and tickles so that soon the boy and dog were laughing and chasing each other around the condominium.

When things had settled a bit, they organized. Jenna set Zoë's bowls out and looked in the fridge. It was woefully understocked. She'd have to go grocery shopping. Étienne suggested that she go the next day in a taxi with Philippe and they could just order from the deli for tonight. "But I have to work tomorrow", she reminded him. "Oh no", he replied, "I've added the next few days to your holidays. Muriel will do your work. She was happy to get a chance to try some new tasks. None of us are indispensable at work."

They ordered food and fed the dog and Philippe and Jenna bundled up and took him out. The parkette belonging to the building was lovely and it had a small playground. Philippe had a quick swing, oblivious to the cold, while the dog stood wagging her tail. The food had arrived when they got upstairs and they sat together at the chrome and glass table eating and chatting. Then it was bath time for Philippe and into the crib, which he'd agreed to for one night. His dad came in to read and many stories later, Philippe was fast asleep.

Meanwhile, Jenna went to unpack her bags and find her toothbrush. The spare room was lovely and she had her own bathroom set up with towels of all sizes and bottles of every possible product she could desire. The bed looked warm and cozy and her feet sank into the carpet. "Coming up in the world, my dear." She said to herself. "No winter draft howling through the window tonight and no jukebox!" When she came out, Étienne was busy on his laptop, so she tidied the toys away, put another load of Philippe's new clothes in the washer, and started on a grocery list. She loved making lists and there was a lot to be done to organize Étienne and Philippe.

Jenna was very aware of Étienne sprawled out on the sofa in his pajamas, busy typing away on his laptop. He, however, seemed barely aware of her presence. Her list complete and even tentative menus made for the next three days, Jenna looked around the room, her eyes coming to rest on the monstrosity in its centre. "Étienne," she queried, "Is there any chance that we could get rid of this multi-tiered coffee table? The sharp edges scare me with Philippe and the dog running around and it's taking up major play territory."

Étienne threw back his head and laughed despite Jenna's shushing. He jumped up and pulled her into a big hug. "Mon petit chou, I agree it must go but could you call MOCCA? It's an art gallery. I'll write the number down here. Ask them if they'd like it in return for a charitable tax receipt." He cupped her cheek with his beautifully sculptured hand and turned serious. "Thank you Jenna. Whatever you decide, I appreciate this support. But please choose us. Choose the life we can build together. Sweet dreams." She wished him goodnight in her gentle voice and he went down the hall on the opposite side which had two doors. She supposed one was his study as he'd gone in and out with his work materials.

Jenna read in a warm bath scented with organic oils, towelled herself off, got into her nightie, and climbed into the king size bed after piling the many extra pillows on the closet shelf. She tried to discipline her mind to review the choices before her but the comfort of the mattress and the luxurious smoothness of the sheets and the warmth of the duvet lulled her to sleep within minutes of her switching off the pretty bedside lamp. Much to her amazement, she woke with the first weak light of the December morning, feeling rested and eager to start the day.

Tuesday looked to be bright and sunny, but well below freezing so Jenna dressed warmly, braided her hair, and set off to get Zoe from Philippe's room and take her out. Zoe was not there, nor was she in the living room. Jenna realized Étienne must have taken her out so she took off her sweater, pushed up the sleeves of her long-sleeved cotton T-shirt, made coffee and toast, scrambled the two eggs in the fridge, and broiled the tomatoes and vegetables that had come with their deli order the night before. She was just finished setting the table, when Étienne came in, and she greeted him with a warm smile. He paused, looking like he was about to pounce on her but settled for a cheerful good morning when Philippe started yelling from his room. Jenna reminded Étienne to feed Zoe, and went and scooped Philippe up, calmed him down, took him to the bathroom, and carried him to the kitchen to kiss his dad. Philippe said, "Look, I get to be a baby, if I want. Mommy never carried me 'cause she said it mussed her up." Étienne took the little boy from Jenna and settled him in a chair saying, "Jenna is not the mussable type." Jenna sniffed, not sure if that was a compliment or not. All her life, she'd been the practical one.

After breakfast, Étienne started to help clean up but Jenna told him she was happy to do the tidying. She was at home and he had to work and, besides, she enjoyed domesticity. Étienne went and got ready to go. He brought Jenna his credit card, told her its code, and gave her $200 cash, telling her to keep the card for now. "Look around the house and order whatever we need. The cleaning lady, Olga, has a key and she'll be in later this afternoon. She comes twice a work to do a thorough cleaning. And don't forget to call about getting rid of the coffee table." He smiled like a man who was free and happy, pulled her braid, kissed her soundly and winked, swung Philippe around and was gone, promising to be back by six.

"Well, sir." Jenna said to Philippe. "You can play while I clear breakfast, then I'll help you get ready, we'll load the last of your new clothes into the washing machine, arrange your drawers and closet and then take Zoe out. It will be 9 o'clock by then and I'll make a phone call so we can get rid of this table and make room to play and then we get to go shopping. We have to pick a nice bed for you!" Philippe caught her enthusiasm and clapped. Soon they were on their way to the furniture store where they managed to wrangle same day delivery and then to the grocery store in another taxi. Jenna sat pointing things out to Philippe and thinking how little one could ever know of what life has in store.

When they returned, the taxi driver agreed to help them with the many bags of groceries and accepting the payment and tip told her it was a pleasure to help such a lovely mommy. She knew she could never replace Philippe's mom, but no child could ever have too much love.

The day passed quickly and when Étienne opened the door at 6:15, Philippe came running, got a big hug and told his dad to hurry and see the new living room. The table was gone and the sofa and chairs had been pulled closer together. The wall between the two big windows was clear and Philippe had lined up all his toys there. "Now we can play cars!" he said, and his dad said "Give me five minutes and I'm ready." "No, no." said Jenna "Dinner is ready. You guys get to eat first and then take the dog out and then you can play and show Daddy your new bed!"

Étienne ate every bite of the stew she had made mopping up the gravy with the homemade no-knead bread he had watched her start the night before with just flour and water and yeast. While enjoying a second helping he asked what the art gallery had said. Jenna replied, "How could anyone consider a jagged coffee table either art or furniture? They were so excited when I sent them a picture and sent someone over right away to evaluate it. They left a charitable receipt for you and asked if they could take the coffee table away right then. I said, of course. Look how much room there is now! Maybe I am boring?" Étienne smiled and cupped her chin with his large, gentle hand and said, "Practical and cautious win out over drama any day in my books. You look very pretty. You had a good day?"

Later that evening, Étienne set his laptop aside and turned to Jenna. She gazed at him, suddenly shy. "Have you made up your mind, Jenna?" he asked and she frowned. Had he meant just 24 hours when he had said she had time to think about it? Really! "I'm a businessman and perhaps too blunt but I'm determined," he went on. "Even after one day I'm more convinced than ever that we can create a happy home and that all of us would benefit and be happier. I hope you will marry me."

Jenna paused, "If I marry you, I would want it to be for good. I mean for life." Étienne gave a somewhat bitter smile, "Oh yes, I think we both had enough of sex and lies. Romance has been disillusioning. Friendship and commitment are what we both want. It is not so? Pour toujours et à jamais."

Jenna closed her eyes. Where was the warmth that had been building between them in Argentina? She was certain she had not had enough romance or sex, but she felt that the right answer was "yes" and so, with a sigh, she held out her hand and said, "Yes, I'll marry you." Étienne kissed her hand and then both cheeks, "Cherie, We will be happy and Philippe too. Do you have questions for me?"

"What about work? I'm in the middle of a project." Étienne played with her fingers. "Forget about work. I can support you. Chelsea's been itching for promotion. She can take over your position."

"What if I want to work?" Jenna asked belligerently. Étienne kissed her hand. "Then, of course, you can work. Tell me how many hours a week and we will get a nanny." Jenna paused thinking of Philippe and Zoe and all the transitioning and replied, "If you can afford it, I'll stay home for at least six months. What about your family?"

"They'll love you and I want them to meet you soon but what do you say to a quick town hall wedding and then you meet them after the holidays? My parents and brother have gone to Belize and my sisters have gone to Florida with their kids, but, perhaps, next year, we can gather and have a traditional family Christmas in Quebec?"

Jenna's childhood dream of a beautiful bridal gown was set aside and she agreed that they could marry quietly. "I'll make arrangements then. Buy a pretty dress. I can ask Mrs. Bond to be witness. Just leave everything to me."

Jenna blinked. "Don't worry, mon lapin," he said, "I have thought more seriously about this marriage than almost any decision I've ever made. I've been thinking about this longer than you realize. It will work. Go and sleep on it." Jenna did and was asleep almost as soon as she laid her head down.

The next morning they ate together again and Étienne asked if she and Philippe could arrange for a Christmas tree and gifts. Buoyed up with the excitement of the season, they spent the day choosing a tree and arranging its delivery, picking out ornaments and gifts and making plans for Christmas. Jenna had always been rather scornful of people spending money freely so she made wise choices and steered Philippe towards durable purchases. Even so, they had a wonderful collection of bags and boxes when they arrived home to make dinner. Philippe was whiny by then and demanding to get the tree up right away, but Jenna was firm and encouraging and he agreed that the next day would be tree day.

They told Étienne at dinner and he said he would come home for the afternoon to help decorate and, perhaps, Jenna would like to go out and buy her dress alone? The next evening Jenna's dress hung in her closet and the tree was up, twinkling with lights and ornaments. Jenna was arranging the prettily wrapped gifts under the tree and trying to keep the dog away from everything. They promised Philippe that the next day he'd sit on Santa's knee to tell him what he wanted and that he could open one of the gifts under the tree on Christmas Eve. Étienne asked her about the gift from Nisha. He asked where Nisha lived and whether she had seen her recently, etc. He put Philippe to bed while Jenna tidied up.

Just as Jenna was about to go to bed, Étienne stopped her with a smile. I have a gift for you he said. "But it's not Christmas yet." she answered. He handed her a small jewelry box. Feeling shy, she opened it, gasping at the lovely solitaire in an old-fashioned setting. "It's an original 1920s piece from the Eaton family. I hope you like it." He took her hand and slid the ring on. "I love it," she said, a tear rolling down her cheek. He kissed the tear away and began to kiss her in earnest. She was just about to join in when he apologized, drew back, framed her face with his hands, and said good night strolling off to his room. Jenna shook off her vague disappointment. Sitting in the deep bath, frequently pausing to watch the dramatic light reflected from the beautiful Asscher cut diamond, Jenna felt content about the future.

Jenna woke early in the morning, took Zoe out, and came back to find Étienne with a mug of coffee ready for her. "We're getting married today." he said and watched her to see her reaction. Surprise, annoyance, and then anticipation crossed her face. "Not too scary", he said. "I wasn't sure I could arrange everything for today but things have worked out. Our ceremony is at 11 o'clock at City Hall." "Why not?" Jenna replied with a smile, "Eggs?" Étienne grinned and said, "Yes, please and then I'll hang out with Philippe and get him dressed and you can get ready."

At 11 o'clock they entered the wedding chamber at City Hall. Jenna looked lovely in her ivory dress and high heeled tango shoes with her long hair hanging down her back in a honeyed curtain. Mrs. Bond gushed over her and her ring and then Jenna saw Nisha, giving her the peace sign, and then running to hug her. "Étienne flew me in for the wedding and lunch and then I fly back. I'm so glad I could be here. I have smudged the room to purify it and I will offer both of you symbolic foods as part of the ceremony." Philippe loved the traditional offerings and Nisha let him help with everything. Jenna felt a sense of peace and beauty, but she was also nervous and she hardly knew what was said. She was glad that Étienne had hired a photographer. She would enjoy the pictures afterwards.

Jenna was very aware of the tall, solemn man holding her hand firmly in his own. He looked impossibly handsome in his wool suit and she had been so pleased to see he had worn his tango shoes too. If she had had to describe Étienne's kiss on the pronouncement that they were man and wife, she would have used the word reverent. She had felt adored and offering him her lips, she made a silent commitment to cherish him for the rest of her life.

Congratulations were said and they were off to a table at the Royal York. Over Muskoka mushroom bisque, Cobb salad, Togarashi spiced salmon, and a sirloin burger for Philippe, Jenna relaxed. It was done. She was married to a man she'd known just two months and she was stepmom to the little boy who was walking around the table advising each person on what to eat. Suddenly, she smiled and turned to Étienne, who searched her face and then called for a final toast to his bride as their crème fraiche panna cotta and coffee arrived.

Just when Jenna thought they would all be heading out an MC announced to all the diners that in celebration of a wedding a special dance would be held. A curtain was pulled back and a small band was revealed instruments at the ready. A hush fell as the romantic strains of Uno by Mariano Mores began and Étienne bowed and held out his hand for hers. He led her to a space cleared in front of the band and swept her into the dance. His eyes held hers and they moved as one to the music. All of Jenna's reservations were gone by the time the music ended and they acknowledged the appreciative applause of the other diners. She smiled at Étienne and said, "Our wedding tune." He replied by kissing her soundly to more clapping.

Back at the apartment, after dropping Nisha at the Island Airport, Jenna wondered what would happen next. Étienne suggested that they relax at home and enjoy Christmas Eve and Christmas Day together. Jenna would put the turkey in, they would go to church, and then have a special meal together the next afternoon.

Stuffed from the turkey dinner and happy from Philippe's joy of Christmas, they lazed about the next evening. Suddenly Étienne turned to Jenna, "I own a house on Kempenfelt Bay in Barrie. I bought it when I first started doing well. I've asked Jason if he can take over my work for a week. Shall we take Philippe there? It won't be a honeymoon, but I just don't feel that it's really winter here in town and we should all get to know each other. You might find it rather primitive."

Jenna laughed, "You can't scare me. North and simple are always good for me. The city is new to me and you're right - where is all the snow and ice?"

Étienne responded, "One day, you'll see northern Quebec in winter. For now, let's go up after breakfast tomorrow and stay till the day after New Year's. You're tired. Go have a bath and I'll put Philippe to sleep and take the dog out. Go to bed." She got up obediently, hesitated as she was unsure if she should kiss him, and then trotted off at his avuncular "Night-night. Philippe say night to Jenna and give her a big kiss from both of us." As Jenna walked to her room, she said to herself, "What if I'd been planning on saying I was ready for my marital rights? After all we've been married two whole days!"

Chapter Five

The next morning they packed a suitcase each. They realized they would need to make a shopping trip after they arrived. They needed food supplies but also had toboggans and helmets on the list. Jenna had shown Philippe a YouTube clip of tobogganing and he had begged to go right away.

It was one of those odd late December days. Only small patches of snow clustered on the landscape, yet a dull weight filled the sky. The clouds were heavy and gray and shouted out to the observant that snow was coming. The drive north to Barrie was a little over an hour.

They spent the time singing. First, Jenna led them in an endless version of "My eyes are dim, I cannot see" to which they added their own verses. The song was meant to be silly and Philippe laughed happily when there were turtles wearing ladies girdles in the store. Jenna laughed, remembering also finding it funny as a child despite having no idea what a girdle was. Jenna's Granddad had fought in Europe in World War II and he had sung all the old army songs when they had car drives. When Jenna's voice tired, Étienne started into Frère Jacques and Alouette.

The roads were clear and they made good time. "It is so easy to have fun with you." Étienne told Jenna, "I have gotten too far from my childhood - not in years but in life. Can I also be your child and regress? I need to bring back the glory of nothing more complex to yearn for than a good packing snow." Jenna replied without hesitation, "Yes, isn't this wonderful? My two boys are going to have so much fun. Let's hope for a good snow!" She was willing to wait for a different relationship. They stopped at a shopping center as they entered the town of Barrie and soon were all ready for the winter holiday.

Jenna craned her neck when the Lake Simcoe shoreline came into sight. A newcomer might find the gray of the lake and the dull grays and browns of the land forbidding but, for Jenna, being able to gaze out over miles of nature, without a single tall building in sight, was freedom. Philippe looked at the large lake with interest and promised Zoe swimming next summer. Presently the car slowed and turned into a long lane with dark pines standing sentinel along its sides. Jenna had no idea what to expect with regards to the house as Étienne had seemed reluctant to say much.

At the end of the gravel drive there was a clearing with the lake, heavy and dark, providing a background for a cheerful, cottage-like house. Étienne got out and went around the car, opening Jenna's door and then helping Philippe out of his car seat. Philippe shouted, "I want to see the water!" Étienne laughed and said, "A true Canadian, eh? Can't wait to be near the shore. Come guys. Let's salute Lake Simcoe before we go inside."

They walked around the house, passed a big fire pit, and went down three steps to the shore. A long dock sat in the water to the right and on the left the next house was at least 150 meters away. Jenna said, "Breathe. Can you feel the energy of the land? Thank you so much for bringing us." And she tiptoed up and kissed Étienne's cheek. They walked to the end of the dock and surveyed the grey waves. Neither of them were daunted by the fierce cold and winter bleakness. In fact, Jenna felt exhilaration at the smack of the waves onshore and the biting wind. "Quentironk," said Étienne, "It means beautiful waters. The First Nations had the name right. This five acres on the lake was my dream but I have hardly been here these past eight years. Let's go see how the house has survived my neglect. I came in the late fall and set the solar panels to keep it at 18° so the pipes wouldn't freeze and burst and so it won't be too cold inside. Let's race to the front door."

Étienne unlocked the beautiful door made of reclaimed antique hardwood and ushered them into the house. He suggested Jenna and Philippe take off their winter stuff and look around and he would start unloading. Once they'd hung their coats and lined up their boots on the snow mat, Jenna and Philippe headed down the short hall into the main room. The wall before them was all window. Jenna knew that she would spend many mornings and evenings in the chair by the window watching the lake. She had come home.

There was a kitchen separated from the big room by an island, and on the left up a shallow set of two stairs, were three large bedrooms with two of them furnished, each facing the lake, and across the hall from them a bathroom, a laundry room, and a mudroom with a side door. To the other side of the great room was another full bathroom and a steep set of winding metal stairs leading to a half room with a balcony that looked down on the front room. "Jenna, I want to sleep here." said Philippe after she had followed him up the staircase. "No, sweetie," said Jenna. "This room is only for kids that are at least seven. You can move up here then. I think you and daddy will be downstairs and I'll sleep up here. Need to pee?" Philippe did and they entered the bathroom where Jenna studied the directions for the composting toilet and held Philippe up to pee. "We need a step for you buddy. What a big high toilet! Look it doesn't flush like usual. We have to put a scoop of stuff in it and wind here but this way we are saving water." Philippe loved the toilet and Jenna saw many unnecessary trips until the novelty wore off.

They went to help Étienne and Jenna saw his look, hopeful but worried. "Mon chou, what do you think? Can you manage here?" Jenna looked at him in amazement, "Manage? I can more than manage. Good luck getting me back to the city! It's perfect. I love it." Étienne sighed with relief and gave her a hug. He released his lingering disappointment over Clarisse's damning condemnation of the house the one time she had visited. Jenna loved it.

They put away the groceries and unpacked their clothes. Jenna admired the furnishings and Étienne explained that a carpenter from his hometown in Québec had built all of it. It was all made out of century-old vintage lumber. "It'll last several lifetimes. Étienne informed her, "But maybe you find it too simple?"

"No." said Jenna. "I find it real. I want to touch it each time I pass. I can imagine many years from now you will see the grooves our hands have made on the back of this chair. We do need some quilts and afghans and cushions to make everything homey though." "Order away, ma cherie. I await your womanly touch." said Étienne with a gleam in his eyes and a rakish grin. Jenna blushed and said she had to make tea and sandwiches and start the chicken simmering for soup. Étienne showed her how to send electricity to each appliance as it was needed. "We are completely off the grid here." he said. "It was more expensive to build but we save now. The only challenge would be if we had no sun for solar power for more than three days."

Philippe set his toys up in the living room and then stared out to the water. "Let's catch fish, Dad. Do you know how?" Étienne replied, "I do indeed mon fils. Shall we try our hands at it? I have a license for fishing. Do you want us to wait so you can come after lunch Jenna?" Jenna said she preferred to organize. She made sure they dressed warmly as the thermometer now read -13°C. "You have 45 minutes maximum." she warned pressing her hand to her heart in joy as she watched father and son lumber down to the dock, supplies in hand, with Zoe skipping beside them. The sun was setting as they returned with a pair of gorgeous yellow perch. "I'll fry these up for dinner after you clean them." said Jenna and prepared three plates to dip the fish in: one with flour and salt and pepper, one with eggs, and one with cracker crumbs.

After a happy dinner at the big wooden table they played the card game "Go Fish" and then Étienne said he would work. He had brought an Internet stick and after logging on became lost to them, hardly even noticing their good nights. "This won't do", said Jenna, but Étienne just smiled and said he would just be a few more minutes. Jenna wished there was some way to keep him away from work a bit more. She went off to bed alone, wrapping herself in the blankets, and sleeping at once.

Jenna woke the next morning to the sound of Philippe clambering up the stairs. "Careful buddy," she said wondering how she had overslept. She tried to look out of the small window behind her bed but it was plastered with snow. She scooped Philippe up for a hug and looked out over the railing to the big window. There was no view of the lake this morning, just a swirling eddy of thick snow. "Let's go pumpkin. Zoe won't stop barking till we get back downstairs. Has she been out?" Philippe squeezed her cheeks as she negotiated the stairs with him, "Daddy and I tried to take her but she would only pee by the door. She doesn't like 'blizars' at all". Jenna turned to Étienne who was exiting the washroom in his pajama bottoms revealing a fine-looking torso for a man his age. "Is it a real blizzard?" she asked blushing when he winked at her. "Yes ma'am," said Étienne with a kiss for each of them. "Environment Canada has issued a winter storm warning and the police have asked drivers to stay off the road. There have already been over 40 accidents in Barrie alone."

"Snowstorm," said Jenna with a certain amount of glee, "Did you get the storm of the century in Québec?" As they breakfasted, they told Philippe stories of winter drama and then built a cosy fire in the wood stove. Étienne declared an official pajama day and Jenna called for a no office work-at-all day. Étienne said he would set a notice on his email after he answered the messages already in. Étienne made delicious crêpes with jam and cheese for lunch. That afternoon, in between games of "Go Fish," cuddling together on the sofa watching the Princess Bride on the laptop, and a few brief forays to take the dog out and measure the snowfall, they became a family unit. Jenna had felt this settling in before when a new foster child finally knew they had found a home for however long it was needed. The day was a happy one.

By nightfall, huge fluffy flakes were falling gently and Étienne promised some tobogganing the next day out on the two feet of fresh snow. They all went off to sleep at nine and Jenna imagined the next day as she fell asleep. It was funny how she didn't miss work at all after more than a decade of it being the centre of her life. "Strange," she thought as she drifted off, "I am happy here at home."

The snow was still falling steadily and the wind was up the next morning when Jenna came out of the shower and sat drying her hair by the wood stove. The boys were undaunted by the delay in tobogganing as the snow would be even better and deeper later in the day. Zoe was even more reluctant to go out and they joked about her sensing a worse storm coming. Another day passed in the house and Jenna surveyed the supplies. They still had flour and other baking basics as well as another frozen chicken but had only bought for three days and there had been no food in the cottage. She sat by the window finally realizing they had not been respecting the possible power of nature and this winter storm. "How's the reserve power?" She asked Étienne, "Have we taken anything in these last two days?" Étienne frowned, "No, we haven't harvested anything to add to the fuel cells so they are draining." he replied. "I didn't want to worry you but we should cook what we need to on the stove now. We can use the wood stove for cooking tomorrow. We have enough wood here for a day and I'll head out to the wood pile and bring more. Come on mon grand. Let's get wood and pull it back on the toboggan."

After one load Étienne and Philippe stood at the door, their forms barely visible under the clinging snow and Étienne said that was enough for Philippe as they could barely see and it was getting colder. He asked Jenna to get him a rope from the mudroom and tied one end to his waist and the other to the door. "It's serious out there now," he said. "I've never seen the like and the wind is really picking up." Jenna waited anxiously as he dragged back three more loads of wood. She and Philippe piled it carefully on the plastic tablecloth they'd laid down a few feet from the wood stove. No light came in from the snow-covered window and she'd switched on lamps placing one right up against the big window by the back door. It was morning, yet as dark as night. Jenna placed her hand on Philippe's warm little head and tousled his hair. They would be smart and be fine.

Étienne came in and Jenna peeled his scarf and hat and mitts off and then helped him with his coat. His hands were near frozen and she pulled off his boots and bundled him onto the sofa telling Philippe to rub his Dad's hands. Covering him with the big blanket off his bed, she made a note to get more blankets soon. They had only three in the house.

They had crepes again for dinner, finishing off the jam and planned the menu for the next day. "I'll make biscuits and we can have the chicken and mashed potatoes for a late lunch and then chicken soup and sandwiches for dinner." said Jenna.

"Sounds perfect," said Étienne. He wasn't really worried about being snowed in. Jennifer and Philippe were safe beside him and they would manage. He did wish that he had brought snowshoes and together they brainstormed supplies to winter-proof the cottage for future years.

The next three days passed and they learned to plan and compromise and ration together and when on the sixth day of the storm they woke to brilliant sunshine, they hooted and hollered and ran around the living-room together, shouting that they had conquered the wilds. They were down to their last supplies but the temperature was rising rapidly and the ping-ping of water dripping from the trees and roof heralded a melt. They drank the last of the coffee as they watched the snow slowly collapse from its meter high level. It was New Year's Eve and they celebrated with the last of their food, saving just enough bread and honey for breakfast the next morning. As they washed the dishes, Étienne pulled the clip from Jenna's hair and buried his face in it. "Wear it down at home, amour."

At midnight Étienne kissed Jenna till she understood what the romance novels meant by senseless. Her body was a quivering, heavy, warm mass of wanting. Étienne set her away from him and told her she'd best be off to her room before he ravished her. She lay in bed enjoying the taste and feel of him that lingered on her senses then cradled her pillow and went to sleep. It was cold in the cabin rooms with just the woodstove but she'd always slept well like that.

By early afternoon on New Year's Day the reports said the highways were clear and after a great struggle, they got the car to the road and set off to the city. The month of January was a busy one for Étienne at work but they settled into a way of being together that was peaceful and occasionally joyous. "Really," thought Jenna, "An arranged marriage isn't such a bad thing."

Chapter Six

The weeks passed and their new family developed a rhythm. Following Mrs. G's principles, Jenna kept everyone well-rested, fed healthy food, and stimulated just enough to be learning. She was the happiest she had ever been and she hugged this knowledge to herself like a warm blanket.

She knew Étienne was watching her sometimes, enjoying her smile and sense of humor, and if a few things were missing like romance and love and sex, she wasn't going to dwell on that. If they didn't love each other at least they were developing the best friendship of their lives. Étienne and she had agreed on that the night before. She had gone to say goodnight to him and he had brushed the hair from her face and said, "I can't tell you how thankful I am to be married to my best friend." She went to sleep on that late February evening, feeling content, only to be awoken shortly after midnight to Étienne's voice by her bed.

"Jenna, sorry. I've had a call from Montréal. There's chaos and a revolt over the implementation. It looks like it's failing. There is a plane waiting for me." He paused, his eyes settling on the nipple of her right breast which was exposed by the wide neck of her nightie. He swallowed visibly and said, "I'll be back in a few days." Jenna struggled to be fully awake but understood absolutely when he asked, "Can I touch you?" She said, "Yes." and felt his fingers brushing over, then moving around her nipple until she felt his hand cupping and feeling the weight of her breast. He sat his bag down, saying, "I know we can't have a quickie for our first time, but you have to tell me to go or I won't be able to." "Stay," Jenna said and revelled in the masculine smoothness with which he tossed aside her blanket, unbuttoned and pulled down his pants, and then lifted her nightie up over her hips. His eyes checked the eagerness in her eyes, her soft lips, and her rapid breathing. Pulling down her undies, he was in her with one swift motion. Half on the bed and half standing, he pulled her hips into position and plunged with a grunt into her. She moaned and grabbed his shoulders and torso, triumphing in the feel of him being finally inside her. He was thrusting faster and faster. She could almost catch his rhythm but he was really aroused and was grabbing her buttocks and thrusting eagerly. With a triumphant grunt and shuddering moan he stilled and then spilled himself into her with a few last strong thrusts. "Ah. Ah." he said, "Death and heaven all in one." And he kissed her all over her face and neck and caressed and kissed each breast in farewell. He pulled himself out and away from her and looking not at all repentant, left her saying, "I'll be back in a few days for more, my wife, finally my wife."

Jenna lay absolutely still, trying to capture and hold onto the smell and feel of him and the warmth spreading out from between her legs. She felt heady with the joy of having been one with him and the sound of his final words, "My wife." She felt completely and utterly happy to be lying in bed, having just joined with her husband, the man she respected and cared for and was beginning to realize she loved. The word love no longer scared her with its potential for loss and she had almost felt the words "I love you," trip off her tongue as he had left. She lay reliving each moment and, within minutes, she was asleep in a tangle of blankets and scents.

The next morning she woke at seven, showered happily and still humming changed the sheets and loaded them into the washer. She put on coffee and put out milk and cereal just as Philippe trotted into the kitchen. "Daddy didn't take Zoe out this morning. She was still in my room," he said.

"I know," said Jenna. "You and I have to run down with her now. Daddy had to go away for work for a few days. Run and pee. Quickly, Zoe needs to pee too." They threw their winter clothes over their pajamas, took the dog out, and came back for breakfast. After breakfast, they colored together for a while and then headed down for a swim. Jenna floated near Philippe in the pool, reliving again the glory of the night before. She smiled at the little boy who was now so dear to her. There was even a small chance that one of Étienne's sperms and one of her eggs had both been ready. Trying not to hope, she still imagined how joyous it would be if they had conceived a baby.

The day passed in a blur of happiness for Jenna. She hoped for a text or call from Étienne but knew he was in the midst of a work crisis. She still thought he could have sent a few words but her concern dissolved when the Concierge called up to say they were admitting a delivery and a huge bouquet of mixed flowers arrived with a note that said simply, "Mine." She and Philippe found a vase and set the flowers out on the new coffee table with its cubbies for his toys underneath. She went to bed, her whole body humming with joy and anticipation. She couldn't wait for Étienne to return home.

The next morning after their swim, Jenna brushed her wet hair and then started making homemade meatballs and pasta sauce. Dressed in an old T-shirt and yoga pants, she hummed as she worked. Philippe occasionally called out to her from his Lego and she would answer.

There was a sound at the door. It was opening. Jenna turned down the burners on the stove. It had to be Étienne but when she rounded the corner to the entrance, her confused mind tried to take in the vision of Clarisse, gorgeous in a bright red coat and hat. She had a suitcase at her feet and more suitcases in the hall which she picked up and sat beside the first. Clarisse said, "I hate travelling alone," removing her hat to display hair that was as perfect as a magazine advertisement, "Bonjour ma chérie, comment est mon plus cher? Come Philippe, kiss mommy." Philippe went happily over and got a kiss and casual praise for his Lego creation. Clarisse turned to Jenna, "Hello, I'm Clarisse. Your name?" "Jenna," Jenna replied.

"Can you take my bags to the spare bedroom? And then I'd love a coffee." Clarisse said with a condescending smile. "Actually, I'm in the extra bedroom." Jenna said gesturing towards where Clarisse had indicated. "Ah, well then, just put me in the master bedroom. I'm back." said Clarisse. "But Étienne sleeps there." said Jenna. "Silly woman," said Clarisse, "I'm his wife. Just take my bags there.

"No," said Jenna, "I am his wife." Suddenly Clarisse's smiling countenance turned disbelieving and then vicious, "No, you're the nanny. You must be. Ah-ha. If you're married, why are you in the spare room?" Jenna stabilized herself with a deep breath, "Étienne and I married five weeks ago. Please come in." Clarisse looked Jenna up and down, taking in the baggy t-shirt and stretchy pants, "Well, my plans have changed. My new marriage isn't working out. I decided to come back. I'll just put my own bags in my old bedroom. That's the master bedroom by the way." She actually sneered at Jenna, turned, tossed her hat and coat on the sofa, and moved her bags in two stages to the master bedroom.

Jenna grabbed her phone, texted Étienne furiously, made sure the volume on her cell phone was on, chatted with Philippe to try to normalize the situation for him, and then went to rescue the pasta sauce. "Whatever next?" she mumbled to herself as she stirred. "Whatever next?"

Chapter Seven

Étienne texted back asking her to hold down the fort till his return late that night. Jenna sighed. Life was such a series of highs and lows but she believed the lows could be managed with deep breaths and steady purpose.

She made a tray with coffee and cake and took it to the living room. Clarisse floated into the room casting herself theatrically on the sofa and then suddenly sitting up shrieking, "Where is the Lenow?" When Jenna asked her what a Lenow was, Clarisse hissed, "Where's the coffee table? What have you done to this room?" Jenna smiled hesitantly, "We gave the table away so we could create a family space." "Well, you're a fool several times over." said Clarisse. "That table was a masterpiece. This place looks like a day-care now."

Jenna felt her blood rising and had to curb the desire to engage in a fight. She sat down on the floor helping Philippe make a Lego farm while Clarisse sighed and muttered and kept complaining that Étienne was not responding to her texts. The long day passed slowly complicated by Clarisse's insistence that the nasty little dog not touch her and the draining need to listen to Clarisse calling every person she knew to let them know she was back in Toronto for a little holiday and staying with her dear Étienne and sweet baby Philippe. By Jenna's calculation, she'd have no time to see her son with all the lunch and dinner dates she was committing to.

After finally getting a wound up Philippe to sleep and walking Zoey, Jenna lay in her bed straining for the sound of Etienne's return. Shortly after eleven, she heard Clarisse's raised voice and the low rumble of Étienne's deep tones. Ten minutes later there was a knock at her door and Étienne entered, set his suitcase down, tossed his jacket on her chair, and sat on the bed pulling her into his arms. "I'm so sorry. Was it a challenging day? Is there anything we can picnic on in here? I'm famished."

Jenna made a plate of sandwiches and tea and returned to find Étienne freshly showered and lying back in her bed with a T-shirt on. "Can I sleep with you? My room has been hijacked and, anyway, I have plans to make up for the lack of attention I gave you last time." Étienne's grin promised pleasures and she felt her hands shake on the tray. She showered while he ate and then she put on the lingerie set Mrs. Bond had given them both with a wink at their wedding. Taking a deep breath she walked out of the bathroom, old insecurities making her shy. Étienne lay in the gentle light of the one table lamp he had left on. He held out his arms for her after looking hungrily at her breasts and thighs clearly visible through the light silk. That night they learned the secrets of each other's bodies, finding ways to bring pleasure to each other and to themselves at the same time. Morning found them tangled together and sated.

Étienne tried to get out of bed without waking Jenna but it was impossible and they giggled as they disengaged and got up. Jenna said she didn't want to wash off the night but Étienne smacked her bottom and told her to hop in the shower, promising the next night would be an even better sequel. Showering together quickly so they could see to Zoe and have breakfast with Philippe, they giggled like teenagers.

They started the day in beautiful harmony enjoying crepes with Philippe. Étienne assured Jenna that Clarisse would not need breakfast and indeed she did not emerge until close to noon. It was Saturday and Jenna was thankful that Étienne would be home. She wondered what would happen with Clarisse's situation, but she didn't worry too much. Possession was nine-tenths of the law and last night had convinced her that Étienne was hers.

Things did not develop as she had hoped. Clarisse declared that she needed to stay with them, crying and pouting and begging until Jenna heard Étienne promising that of course she needed to be with Philippe and she was welcome to stay for a while. Étienne explained to Jenna that Clarisse was no longer entitled to support for herself so was threatening to take Philippe if she had nowhere to go. "Let's just wait and see if she patches things up with the new husband. Please Cherie? Life has not been as easy for Clarisse as you might think." Jenna agreed to wait.

An uncomfortable truce developed where Clarisse vied quite successfully for the attention of both Étienne and Philippe but ignored Jenna and made her feel like an intruder in what should have been her home. When Clarisse was out shopping or lunching, Philippe and Jenna created happy times quite successfully and the nights were magical with her and Étienne making love and memories as they cuddled together in the big bed. Even their breathing seemed matched up at night but outside their room they were practically strangers.

Every day, Jenna hoped that Clarisse would be leaving but two weeks went by with Clarisse making more and more demands on Étienne's energy, stressing Philippe out, and making Jenna feel like the maid with a petulant demands for coffee and special foods and quiet. Étienne was often at work or responding to emails and Jenna tried to ensure Zoe and Philippe had peaceful days. She, herself, was content until that moment each morning when Étienne withdrew from her, for he showed no affection for her in front of Clarisse. She felt uncertain when they were together in the living room. Étienne had never told Jenna that he loved her or needed her though he had brought to her body sensations and satisfaction she had never imagined possible. But maybe some men were good at that and he was trying to make Clarisse jealous? Étienne was making love to her without protection but he had never mentioned a hope for a baby. Perhaps he thought she was on the pill? Jenna often found herself staring out over the cold, grey of Lake Ontario wondering how secure she should feel.

It was such a confusing time for Jenna. The harmony she and Philippe had developed was challenged by Clarisse's frequent counter suggestions and spoiling. His behavior was regressing and he liked to lie like a baby in Jenna's arms. Both of them would sigh in relief when Clarisse's taxi would call and she would blow kisses and go off to one of her luncheons. Jenna asked Étienne if she and Philippe and Zoe could go to the cottage but he said he needed to settle some issues with Clarisse before any steps could be made. He was still gentle and kind and caring even arranging that Olga would come in and clean daily and prepare Clarisse's late breakfasts but Jenna could sense he was stressed and worried.

The month of February passed and Clarisse was still installed in the master bedroom. All of Jenna's old insecurities and fears of loss came back and she woke each morning, lacking energy and feeling like a stranger in her own body. After a swim with Philippe, a walk with Zoe, and some yoga, she would feel fine, but the first part of the day seemed to be really draining her.

Finally one evening, Jenna lost her cool. Her period had been a few days late and though she'd forbidden hope, it had arisen. She had started to imagine a little baby. Sadly, its already dear little face was dashed away with the smear of blood she found on wiping. Now, disappointed, tired from the busy day with Philippe and Zoe, and sick of Clarisse's elegant whining, Jenna confronted Étienne when he entered her room. He had spent the evening chatting with Clarisse while Jenna had bathed Philippe and put him to bed.

"What am I? Housemaid or nanny?" Jenna's usually calm disposition was gone. Her rage had built to unreasonable but sturdy proportion and she demanded Clarisse leave the next day. Étienne frowned and replied that he was not going to send his son's mom away, especially not suddenly. "Mon chou, can we just get through this together?" he asked trying to draw her into his arms. But Jenna stormed into the bathroom, turned on the radio, and soaked in the bath for hours adding more hot water when the bath cooled and finally exiting when she couldn't bear to become any more prune-like. Étienne was asleep with the light off and she crawled into bed lying stiff and distressed until she finally fell into a restless sleep.

Immediately on wakening her eyes went to Étienne's bare pillow. She saw with dismay that the morning was well advanced and she jumped up, running into the living room and pausing, bewildered. Clarisse was languishing on the sofa while Philippe, still in his pajamas, played sullenly. Jenna became aware of Zoe whining from Philippe's room and opened the door to find she'd had several accidents. Jenna ran to the kitchen to find it in disarray and no food in Zoë's bowl. After filling it, she re-entered the living room and asked stiffly if Philippe had had breakfast. "Ask him", said Clarisse. "He's old enough to get cereal." Philippe piped up, "I did. I did. I got some but I'm hungry."

"See." said Clarisse, "Your perfect mommy act just couldn't last. You should have known that Étienne would want to be rid of you eventually. The poor man told me again this morning how much he loves me but you just can't let him go, can you? Look at you looking like something the cat dragged in. How can you live with yourself stepping between a man and his wife and son? If he didn't feel so sorry for you he would just ask you to leave but he says you have nowhere to go. Pathetic."

Jenna stood, confused and trembling, remembering the long session of whispering and occasional laughter the evening before. How could she have been so stupid? Thank God she wasn't pregnant. Where would she go? How would she find a new job? Homeless and unloved had never felt so sad. She felt physically sick from the shock and ran to the washroom to throw up. Philippe barely looked at her. Clarisse and Étienne obviously wanted her gone.

Resting her cheek against the cool marble of the tub enclosure, she planned her escape. She would take only what she had come with and be gone within the hour. She rose on shaky legs, brushed her teeth and hair and washed her face. She twisted her hair up into a tight chignon laughing at how proudly she's been wearing it down and swinging it around. "Stupid. Stupid. Stupid." She said to herself, starting a flood of tears.

In her room, her brain could only process practical trivia. She realized she'd have to keep one of the underwear sets as she had tossed her old ones out but, besides that, she packed only her remaining old clothes, Mrs. G's linens, and her sunflower plate in three shopping bags. She would take nothing of Étienne's. She set her rings and his cards and money on the dresser, picked up her purse, and when Clarisse and Philippe were not looking she grabbed her winter stuff from the front hall closet and crept to the door and silently left. There was nothing to say. They could resume their old life and she could file for divorce. She ached at the thought of leaving Philippe and Zoe but forbade her mind from even thinking of Étienne. Marching resolutely into the winter cold, she made for Union Station.

Fortunately, a bus was leaving for North Bay within 20 minutes. The fee was less than she'd spent recently to have a day of fun with Philippe, but now she was counting every penny. As she waited in the small line up on the cold platform, she checked her phone repeatedly. If Étienne would just text or call. If she had misunderstood, they could make everything all right, but no message came through. Unable to resist, she texted Étienne that Philippe was home alone with Clarisse but there was still no response.

She boarded the bus after tying her bags together and putting them in the baggage storage under the bus. Hunger made her nauseous but she hadn't thought to grab anything to eat. The bus would stop several times so she could grab something in Barrie or Orillia. Tears flowed down her cheeks as the bus pulled onto Highway 400 and headed north.

She knew she wasn't going home. Home had become Étienne and Philippe and Zoe. She was just looking for a place to live and knew enough to go to a friend. She had little money to her name and no job. Worse, the thought of never lying warm and content with her cheek on Étienne's chest and his arm holding her close was unbearable. And her worry for Philippe and Zoe and their care was huge. She would send a letter to Philippe every week and Étienne could give it to him. She'd seen too many bewildered kids from whose lives adults had just vanished that she couldn't do that to anyone. Her reasonable planning quickly gave way to anguish. Clarisse was incredibly gorgeous but if Étienne had half a brain he would've stuck with her. She hated his stupidity but at the same time she ached with love for him. How could he not see through Clarisse to her selfish disregard for others? He deserved better. She would have worked hard for their happiness.

Jenna found that even drawing a full breath was challenging. She wrapped her coat and scarf more tightly around herself, pulled her hat low over her eyes and rested her tired head against the window falling into a fitful sleep. The bus stopped in Orillia and she reached for her phone to see if any message had come in. It was gone. The bus driver sympathized but said anyone could've scooped it off the seat beside her while she slept. "Just as well." Jenna muttered to herself. "At least now I won't torture myself with hope." She bought a sad looking egg salad sandwich and some tea and got back on the bus. No more organic apples for her. The cost of one at the bus stop snack bar was more than the sandwich.

The bus driver agreed to drop her at the coffee shop just off the highway before North Bay. A few hours later she collected her bags and crossed the parking lot. Her body ached from the five and a half hour bus ride, her night of restless sleep, and her tension. She had to force herself to cross the almost empty lot to the door. Inside, she sat at the counter in the drab pit stop and ordered the all-day breakfast special. She would wait until someone from the reservation came in and hitch a ride to Nisha. She chatted with the waitress, sharing little herself, but listening kindly to the woman's woes.

After an hour, a family came in who recognized Jenna and asked if she wanted a lift to North Bay with them. When she said she needed to get to Nisha, they drove her there first. Half an hour later she knocked at Nisha's door. The family wound down their car window and called out for her to just go in. Sure enough, the door was unlocked. She waved, entered, and called out. No one was home so she hung her coat and sat down to watch TV as the sun finished setting.

Nisha came in, took one look at Jenna's face and held her tight. Jenna began to sob in earnest and Nisha held her, passing tissue, and encouraging her to cry it out. When Jenna emerged from her sobbing, she saw that Nisha's kids were cooking dinner. Nisha led her to the washroom, told her to have a hot shower, handed her fresh towels, and said she'd be making tea.

Chapter Eight

Over a warm mug of tea and dinner, Jenna begged Nisha not tell anyone that she was there and Nisha agreed that it looked like she needed some time to grieve in peace. They would keep her as long as she needed and she could share Nisha's double bed. After dinner, Jenna was tucked into blankets to sleep soundlessly until morning. She slept through the phone call in which Nisha denied her presence and Étienne's call was not mentioned in the days that followed.

Jenna fell into a routine, helping Nisha with the community programming and knitting with a supportive group of women. She would send the sweater to Philippe. Her tears fell into the wool as she created Zoe on the front. She knitted the difficult pattern with care and love. She knew her letter would have reached Toronto and at the end of the first week started looking for a reply when Nisha brought in the mail. Surely, Étienne would encourage Philippe to draw her a picture? She took time and care with the stories she sent Philippe in her weekly letters. Nisha ushered her out walking every morning and afternoon and she drew strength from the sightings of animals working hard to survive the winter and the big old trees just waiting for spring.

The weather was cold and snowy and though it was soon mid-March, there was no sign of a thaw. No one questioned Jenna or suggested she make plans and she just coasted, getting used to being on her own again and building strength from the kind support she received. Nisha suggested she stay and help her teach. Jenna found that she was very good at encouraging others and explaining things. A number of the youth were interested in the area of health data and she told them about her work in health information management. She was back to her quiet ways. She'd lost the glow and confidence that Étienne's loving had given her. She missed her new family and was shattered that she received no word from them but she slowly grew strong again with the gentle help of her friend.

When the phone rang on a late March morning, she answered it without thinking, hanging up quickly when she heard Étienne's repeated exclamation of her name and his dear voice saying, "Mon dieu. Jenna. Jenna. Jenna. I'm coming there right now."

All Jenna could think of was his wanting a divorce and devoid of reason, she threw on her winter clothes and headed away from town into the forest. She needed to think. She needed space. She was angry at him. "Let him find her if he could!" Foolishly, she kept walking, oblivious to the rapidly strengthening snow and the bitter wind.

The path was well set by the hunters and sleds that headed towards the ice fishing spot in the lake and she trudged along. She'd stop when she reached the cabin by the shore. She was aware of a big, ugly dog following her. She drew comfort from the gaunt-looking beast. She tried to call him to her but he kept pace beyond grabbing distance. She knew she'd best be careful as there were strays on the reserve who were not well-socialized. She pushed onwards, daydreaming of how sorry Étienne would be if she died from the cold and imagining him weeping at her funeral. Revenge fantasies could be so sweet.

Suddenly, Jenna stopped. She must've turned off the path. She had just stepped into snow so deep it entered the top of her right boot. Shaking it out as best she could, leaning against a birch tree, she tried to get her bearings. The snow swirled around her. She was lost in the forest in the late afternoon.

Jenna pulled her scarf more firmly over her nose to lessen the sharpness of the cold that came on the intake of her breath. "Stupid. Stupid. Stupid. Stupid." she said, remembering finding Philippe and she blinked tears from her eyes. What has she been thinking? Who had she been trying to punish? How had she let herself be bitter rather than committed to love?

Jenna called out to the trees to shelter her and struggled to retrace her steps. With care, she should be able to get back to the path, but after endless minutes and missteps, she realized that she could not find her way. She needed to find shelter for the night. It was darkening quickly. She just needed to survive the night and she knew the community would track her in the morning.

When the wind died for a moment, she spotted a large rock outcrop that would block the wind. Briefly she envisioned this spot in summer. She was not too far from the lake. She dug out the snow in front of the outcrop creating a wall of snow three feet high. She pulled off some spruce branches to create a roof.

The dog watched her and she tried sending it for help but it just danced around. It was now dark and Jenna curled into her nest. She tried to create a cocoon of body heat but she started trembling. Suddenly, the dog's face appeared through the branches. She called to him and he climbed gently into the shelter settling his body against hers. She pulled her long hair over her face and brought her hands out of their sleeves and inside her coat tying the sleeves in front. Her feet were already cold but she could think of no solution. She slowed her breath to match the dog's large lungs and managed to relax into a trance. Morning would come. She imagined planting a spring garden as she kept her breath steady. Lying there, she accepted the possibility of death and four words came to her mind like a mantra: faith, hope, love, and charity. She had been lacking in offering all four. She had not given Étienne a chance to talk to her or explain. She fell asleep praying for a second chance.

The snow had stopped falling the next morning and the first thing Jenna registered was the dog's kind brown eyes and then the ping-ping as snow and ice fell from the trees and water dripped. It was a thaw! She rose out of her shelter with renewed hope, telling the dog they would be safe soon. She could hardly feel her feet and fought to keep her balance. Jenna felt bereft when the dog slunk away through the trees, his large frame slowly vanishing from sight.

Jenna followed the dog's footsteps. They were easy to pick out as a crest of snow broke with each step. She would follow him and find help. Her feet started tingling and burning and she knew she had some frost damage. She had to pee and she was very thirsty. "Well, Jenna," she said to herself, "a minute of cold is better than wet pants." She peed and then found an icicle to suck. She forced herself to keep trudging after the dog, counting each step out loud. She christened the dog Jim as he had the same long, lanky, comical look of an actor she adored. Jim was clearly not going back to the path, but taking a shortcut through the forest. She was sure he was heading for the community.

The sudden warmth was both a blessing and a curse. The sun shone and she knew they were at or above the freezing mark. Globs of wet snow fell from the trees hitting her with force and soaking parts of her hood and coat. Her wool mittens were soaked from her many falls and she hung them on a tree branch putting her hands in opposite sleeve ends. What seemed like hours passed as she doggedly followed Jim's path and then she heard the baying of dogs. Someone was near. She tried to yell but knew she would not be heard over the howls and barks. Suddenly, Jim came crashing towards her with a pack of dogs on his heels and the Chief's son running behind on snowshoes. Behind him, she saw Étienne with a group of searchers. "Funny," she thought as she collapsed into a faint, "I'm so happy to see him. Why was I so angry?"

She didn't hear Étienne's words as he ran to her and cradled her in his arms. She came to for a second and heard, "Mom chou. Mon chou." and then she faded away again. The men took turns carrying her back to the trail where they settled her in Étienne's arms on the sled pulled by a snowmobile, and made good time back. They had called for an ambulance and Jenna was taken to the North Bay Hospital oblivious to all the commotion and Étienne's hand holding hers.

Miraculously, she had suffered only mild frostbite on her toes and slight dehydration and exhaustion. The doctor ensured she was settled in, checked the tests they had run, and went out to where Étienne was sitting with Nisha in the waiting room. "I'm Dr. Mohamed. Are you the husband?" he asked. "Yes, how is she?" Étienne replied, grasping the doctor's hand. "She should be just fine. She needs rest and her feet will take a few weeks to heal but they will be completely fine. There's no need to worry about the baby. Everything looks normal. I'll check in with you again when I'm on my next round. You can sit in the room one at a time if you'd like. See you later."

Nisha nodded, "I was pretty sure about the baby from the day that Jenna arrived but was waiting for her to share." She laid her hand on Étienne's arm looking briefly at his stormy face, "Peace," she said but he was gone. He stormed into the hospital room, all his worry coalescing into frantic anger. He shook Jenna's arm and when she opened her eyes, he said, "You fool. How could you risk a life? How could you desert Philippe? How could you pretend to care about me?" Jenna tried to catch his words but they had given her something to ensure she slept and she simply closed her eyes again wondering why Étienne looked 10 years older with new gray hairs and worry lines. She only knew she was safe with him there and she slept.

The next morning, she was settled in a wheelchair by Nisha and taken out the door. There, Étienne waited in his glistening Mercedes. When Jenna started to protest, Nisha said, "I married you with our traditional ceremonies and good medicine, but you must do your part. Harmony can be achieved. Spring is on her way. Welcome the cycle of the seasons. Winter can be hard, I know. I love you. Let me get this buckled. Bye-bye." Nisha shut the door firmly, patted the roof, and Étienne drove off.

Jenna felt a cold, wet nose on her neck and turned to see Jim filling half the backseat. "The Chief said he belonged to you now." said Étienne. "Hi Jim," said Jenna, glad of a safe topic. "He saved my life. His name is Jim."

Étienne told Jim to sit down in the car and said, "I think he might be part wolfhound and part German Shepherd. He's a great guy. He stayed with me at the motel last night. He ate half a bag of food. Once he's got some flesh on his bones, he'll be very handsome. Enough about the dog. Have you got something to tell me?"

Jenna told an increasingly grim-faced Étienne the story of the dog and her night in the forest. He promised the dog a huge reward. The dog thumped his long tail against the door and rested his chin on Étienne's seat. "Try to sleep Jenna. We can talk when you've rested at home." Étienne pulled the blanket around her when he saw that she was asleep. He headed for Barrie.

Chapter Nine

"Hey, sleepyhead. We are home," Étienne said, gently releasing Jenna's seatbelt. She woke up looking around in bemusement. She had been expecting to see the tall buildings of Toronto and then the parking garage at the condo, but they were parked in front of the cottage and Philippe and an older woman were standing in the open doorway.

Zoe came prancing out and Jenna exclaimed happily, sharing a smile with Étienne as he opened her car door and handed her out to an ecstatic Zoe. "I wonder how she'll like Jim," Jenna said, to which Étienne responded, "There's only one way to find out." He opened the rear door and Jim lumbered out, his lazy energy a sharp contrast to Zoë's leaping and barking. "This might be a slow-blooming friendship," Étienne laughed as Jim steadfastly ignored Zoe and went about his business.

Meanwhile, Jenna was walking towards Philippe who stood staring at her. She knelt down in front of him in the front hallway and said, "I'm so sorry that I've been gone. I'm so happy to be with you again." And she waited. Philippe paused and then ran into her arms. Tears poured down Jenna's cheeks as she rocked him and stood up cradling him. "Here, take a tissue. I'm Celine, Étienne's mother. I'm so glad to meet you." Étienne's mother smiled at Jenna. Her French accent, bird-like head tilt, and fluttering hands added music to her speech and set Jenna at ease.

"Come." said Étienne. "Give me your coat. Philippe hop down. We have to get Jenna off her feet. Remember what I said on the phone?" Together they pulled off Jenna's coat and boots, called the dogs in, and walked with Jenna to the great room. She sighed with pleasure at the afternoon sun streaming through the window. "Best take a visit to the washroom and change into the nightie and housecoat I've laid on your bed." said Celine. "I've made Pâté chinois and home-made baked beans so, after you've had some tea, we will eat. I put you in the last room on the right. We ordered a queen size mattress and box spring but you will need to order some furniture."

Jenna glanced at the pile of twenty or so boxes piled up in one corner. "Oh, the beddings and stuff I ordered?" she asked Étienne. 'Yes, I've been waiting so we can sort them together. Off you go." he concluded, unwilling to get into any emotional territory at that time.

There was no sign of Étienne's clothes in the closet that Jenna glanced into. She sighed. Of course they could not just get back into bed together, but how she yearned for the smell of him and the steady beat of his heart under her cheek. She could no longer even recall the anger and angst that had caused her to take off without discussion. How could such negative feelings well up so overwhelmingly? She promised herself that she would practice controlling such negativity. It had almost meant never being here with those she loved ever again.

Jenna was nervous of Étienne's mom and how they would share Philippe. She was somewhat scarred from her experiences with Clarisse, but Celine's somewhat bossy tone and opinions were matched by a happy energy and love and patience. By the time dinner was over, Jenna had relaxed. Philippe was full of information. "Nana brought her cat. It's locked in our room. Me and Nana sleep in the twin beds but we aren't twins. Zoe doesn't know her place. The cat scratched her and she cried. Because Zoe shouldn't jump on old cats. The cat is huger than Zoe and his name is Aldrick. I'll show you."

Jenna closed her eyes at the pleasure of hearing Philippe's happy chatter. She would tread carefully. She would be reasonable and unemotional and maybe with time she could win back Étienne's trust. What must he think of her deserting him? Deserting a child? Suddenly, she snapped back to the conversation. Étienne's mom had switched to English and was detailing her plans. "So, your papa will pick me up tomorrow if you are sure you and Jenna can manage?" Celine looked at Jenna. Étienne was staring intently at her. She could not make out the emotion behind his stare. Jenna blushed making her look lovely as the firelight shone on her rosy skin.

"My mom has been with us since the day you took off. I couldn't just leave work right away so she came to help." Jenna wanted to ask, "What about Philippe's own mom?" but felt ashamed of her own foolishness in leaving so suddenly. What right had anyone to judge? She looked at her hands, took a deep breath and said, "I'm ready to look after Philippe. I would never leave again without discussion."

"Good enough for now," said Étienne clearing his throat. "You go lie on the sofa. You're not supposed to walk too much as your toes heal. I'll bring your hot chocolate over. Philippe, let's take the dogs out. Maman, merci. Dîner était super." Jenna watched as Étienne gave his Mom a big kiss and hug and then stood quietly away from her as she navigated her way to the sofa. Her feet were sorer than before as the pain killer was wearing off. The doctor had suggested avoiding any more medications.

Jenna watched from the window as the two dogs and father and son walked and ran around the shoreline in the darkness. "Please let me help you tidy up," she said to Celine but Celine said, "No, no. I am fine for one more night. I've been having fun caring for these two and hanging out at the lake, but I'll pass the torch back to you gladly after this. Six weeks of le petit singe was plenty for me. I'll be glad to get back to my husband and my painting." Jenna could catch that Celine had referred to Philippe as some small animal and decided then and there to study French.

"Celine, I'm so sorry," said Jenna but his mom replied, "Tut-tut. Not a word. I'm sure you had your reasons, good or otherwise. It'll all come out in the wash. In French, we say vouloir, c'est pouvoir – to want is to be able. As long as you can tell me right now that you love my boys, I can leave happy. I was glad to finally get to be a mémé to Philippe."

"I do love him, love *them*." said Jenna. "I've almost been numb from loneliness and worry. I tried to find peace in myself and accept that I could live my life alone again but there was a void where they needed to be." Celine came over, knelt beside her, and embraced her. "Well then, ma petite maman. You must mend your fences and take care of yourself and them. I'll come back in the summer and the autumn when you will really need my help." Jenna blinked. She really didn't think it would be so tough in the summer, but maybe Celine was thinking of protecting Philippe from the lake.

Celine hung the dish towel. "All tidy. I'm off to shower and then to bed to read. Send the boys to say good night to me."

Étienne and Philippe came in and played cars and Lego. It looked as if all the toys from Toronto were at the cottage now and not once did Étienne check his Blackberry for work messages. The condo and the office seemed a world away.

Jenna lay peacefully on the sofa, half-awake, until Étienne suggested that she take herself off to bed. "What about Philippe?" she asked. "I'm now an expert at Philippe care, c"est vrai my son? Am I not the best at getting you to sleep? My story reading is so bad you fall asleep to avoid it." He swung Philippe upside-down and carried the laughing, wriggling imp over to kiss Jenna good night. "See you in the morning," he said to Jenna and she could feel the caution and reserve in him.

Jenna slept snuggly in the cozy room. She loved sleeping to the sound of waves lapping the shore where the ice was receding. She woke to Philippe yelling, "Papa, can I just open the door and let Jim and Zoe out?

Jenna got dressed. In the drawers, she had found all the clothes that Étienne had bought for her in Montréal and Toronto. She pulled on the beautiful undies and fastened the rose colored bra. How big it made her breasts look. They seem to spill out of the cups. She pulled a lovely sweater over her head and sat down to gently pull the jeans over her bandaged feet. She stood wincing and tried to do up the zip. She could not fasten it. The button was too tight.

Jenna took a hair tie and threaded it over the button, through the hole and over the button again. Mrs. G had taught her how to stretch clothes through growth and weight changes. She remembered her favorite pair of jeans in high school and how they had made them last for years and then made shorts of them. She smiled at herself. She looked plump but happy again. She vowed to start walking as soon as her feet healed. She needed to stay fit. She went to the washroom where she blew dry her freshly washed hair until it hung around her face like a silky shield. She looked pale so she pinched her cheeks and bit her lip.

Entering the great room, she sighed in peace. Étienne's mom greeted her from the stove where she was making what smelled like a mushroom omelette. Étienne was reading on the sofa. Philippe was throwing sticks to the dogs from the back deck. How she loved it here. She was so grateful to be back, close to those that she loved. Somehow, she would make things right.

Chapter Ten

Jenna hesitated in the doorway. She needed to clear the air with Étienne. She had to apologize and explain but there seemed no way to get him alone. She felt she deserved his anger but he looked up at her with a smile and hopped off the sofa telling her to rest her feet and asking if she still wanted tea in the morning or maybe some honey and lemon.

Jenna kissed Philippe and he came and sat with her on the sofa showing her dog pictures on his dad's iPad. "Which kind is most like Jim? Do you think his dad was a wolfhound?" They bent their heads together over the pictures. When Étienne returned with her hot drink, Philippe pulled him down beside them. "Now, that's a picture." said Celine. "A family if I ever saw one." Jenna blushed and looked at Étienne who said, "Well, mon chou. I am happy to be sitting here with you." "Me too," said Jenna, and felt her heart shifting and finding room for hope. She wondered why books didn't describe the sense of expansion that charity could bring.

"Le petite dejeuner is ready." called Celine and they ate, chatting and laughing over the fluffiest omelette Jenna had ever had. "The secret is in the butter," explained Celine. "I add a tablespoon of small cubes of really cold butter to the beaten eggs before adding them to the pan. The butter melts and creates the fluffies." She and Jenna made a pact to cook together on the next visit.

Afterwards Jenna napped on the sofa while the others took the dogs to the vets. Zoe needed a booster shot and Jim was going in for neutering. They came back just before lunch with Zoe. Philippe was excited. "The vet says Jim is probably half Great Dane. He's like Scooby-dooby-do." Jenna hugged him and said, "Well, we have one of the biggest and one of the smallest dogs. What a sight we'll be at the park!"

Étienne made crepes while his Mom packed and they were just sitting down when his Dad arrived. Just as tall and dark as his son, he towered over Jenna, his face revealing nothing. They exchanged pleasantries as they tucked into the food. Then he asked Jenna to recount her adventure in the forest and when he saw her face and eager eyes as she recounted Étienne arriving to the rescue, he patted her hand. "It must've been tough, my dear but you are safe now." He's a kind man Jenna thought. Quiet like his son and a good, steady person.

The sun shone and the temperature sat just above zero. "Spring is here." said Jenna. "Mais non, don't be so sure," said Celine. "March came in like a lamb but shall go out like a lion. We had best head for Québec my dear. We will rest tonight in Québec City. We have a room at Auberge Saint-Antoine. It's an inn within the old city walls. Philippe, you will come and see the fort next year."

There was a bustle of activity as they saw Philippe's grandparents off. Jenna looked forward to their promised visits in May and September. Jenna still hoped for a chance to talk with Étienne but there was a sternness around his mouth that had not been there before and he seemed to be avoiding their being alone.

Over the next few days Étienne prepared the food, tidied, and even did her laundry. When she protested he replied, "The doctor said your body had quite a shock with the near hypothermia and you need to take it easy and recover. We need to take gentle care of you. Just for a few weeks." Jenna sighed with pleasure. She could only faintly remember being so cosseted. It felt so good to be so safe and cared for.

Somehow the opportunity to talk didn't arise and they settled into a friendly but cautious truce as March turned into April and the temperature stayed a few degrees above zero. Jenna started to dream of spring. Étienne had ordered seed and plant catalogs and software for garden design and they spent hours each day planning a one acre organic garden between the road and the cottage. The list of supplies and roses and shrubs and fruit trees and flowers and seeds that they placed orders for grew and grew. Philippe had his own area to design and they planned to plant a quick growing screen of beans around his secret garden.

They had unpacked and washed all the new blankets and towels and cushions that Jenna had ordered during their last stay. They had also selected a gorgeous bedroom set for the spare room in a beautiful cherry wood. Étienne encouraged Jenna to inventory the kitchen and order for it. How she loved comparing patterns and styles! She showed Étienne and Philippe the final options. Together they chose first-class kitchenware. "Stuff to last several lifetimes is what we want." said Étienne and Jenna waited happily each day for the Postal Service to arrive with her boxes.

The dish service by Wedgewood arrived and she almost cried. The pattern of Devon Spring Roses was so perfect. Mrs. G. would have loved it. She had always used the best dishes for her foster kids saying, "What's the use of lovely things if lovely people don't enjoy them?" Jenna had never dreamed of being able to set the table for a family such as she had now. That night they ate their home cooking in style. She knew the situation with Clarisse was still not clarified but Jenna could see Étienne had thrown his oar in with her.

Jenna had asked twice if Étienne needed to go to work but he had replied tersely, "Not at present." She still felt she had no right to probe. She was glad he was home and assumed he had taken holidays while she convalesced.

By mid-April Jenna's feet had healed. Étienne said, "Shouldn't you be going to the doctors?" Jenna replied, "If you think I should, I will." Étienne frowned, "Well, I'm no expert but I certainly think it's a good idea. I can come with you if you want. It seems the responsible thing to do." Étienne continued gazing at Jenna with a frown. She was puzzled. "Well, of course. My family doctor is still in North Bay. I couldn't get one in Toronto." Étienne made a dismissive gesture, "No worries. I will make some calls. I did an electronic medical record installation at a Barrie clinic last year. I'll see if they can take us on as a family."

A few calls later and Étienne had an appointment for her and a check-up for Philippe for the following Thursday. He'd have to go to Toronto that day but he had ordered a new Volvo for Jenna and it would be ready on Monday for pickup. When Jenna had protested, Étienne had said he expected his family to be safe on the roads and that this car had great features. Jenna looked at him sitting with Jim's head resting on his foot. Étienne looked sad and she yearned to run and hold him and make everything better but she had felt she had no right to.

Jenna felt wonderful. She found herself looking hungrily at Étienne's lips and chest and hands. Her body felt strong and fully alive. She hadn't lost any weight or inches. Indeed, she felt fuller than before, but then Étienne had been making sure the injured flesh of her toes had time to heal, and the most she had done was unpack her purchases and organize the house.

She surveyed the rooms. The bedrooms were cosy with her gorgeous quilts and handmade furniture. The kitchen was fully stocked with every pot or dish a cook could require. The living room was lovely. And the two bathrooms were all set. She turned her thoughts to outside. Étienne had ordered a large conservatory/greenhouse to be built alongside the cottage with a glass passage between it and the side door. They would have fresh greens and root vegetables all year as half of the greenhouse would be temperature controlled gardens and half would be a tropical sunroom. Jenna spent hours online searching for a garden set finally settling on a Mennonite set that included an 8-seater divan and a swing. She imagined gently gliding while she and Philippe read stories.

If Jenna could just break through the careful reserve Étienne had towards her, everything would be fine. She had hurt him badly and it showed. That night with Philippe tucked into bed, they sat together but separated by 5 feet of carpet. Jenna bit her lip and twisted a strand of her long hair. Looking up she saw Étienne gazing hungrily at her. Drawn by him, she rose up and knelt before him taking his face in her hands and gently kissing his lips. He thrust his fingers into her hair and kissed her. Her mouth opened hungrily as she wound her arms around his neck, pulling on him, begging him with her movements to be one with her. Étienne's hands moved to her breasts and he weighed them in his hands. "Very nice. Yummy." he said kissing each nipple through her sweater. She untucked his shirt so her hands could feel the bare skin of his back.

Étienne rose up, pulling her to her feet and saying, "We need a bed." Holding her hand and gently kissing her he led her to his room. Undressing her, he pulled back the blankets and feasted his eyes on her swelling curves as he quickly undressed. They made love. There was no other way to describe how they worshipped each other and then satisfied slept wrapped together in the centre of the big bed. Jenna woke later and had to get up but Étienne stopped her. "Don't leave me, please." Jenna kissed his lips, "Just for a moment. I promise." she replied hurrying so she could get back to their warm cocoon.

Morning came and they made love again as the first birds of spring made music outside. "Mine." he said cupping her face. "Mine." he said caressing and kissing her nipples." Mine." he said his hands on her hips pausing before he entered her. "Mine." he repeated as he slid inside her and, "Mine." Jenna replied pushing him so they rolled and she sat atop him rocking, leaning over him, putting one nipple and then another to his lips for sucking till she came and he came and they subsided, gasping and grinning.

That Sunday Étienne finished setting up shelves in the large closet that would be their pantry and the three of them organized all the dry goods and cans they had ordered. It felt so good to have a stock of food carefully arranged. Even Philippe seem to share their growing content. He was growing like a weed and learning new things every day. Jenna loved the evenings getting Philippe ready for bed, making sure the dogs were walked and settled and then that moment when she turned to Étienne and said, "I'll just get a bath." She knew he'd be waiting for her fresh from a quick shower in the second bathroom, and naked under their sheets. Jenna had moved most of her stuff into his room and she never planned on leaving.

Thursday she was sad to see him dressed in a suit again and heading for the city. "Are you starting back to work again?" she asked. "No, I'm going to sign papers. I have sold the company to Jason. I didn't want to say anything till it was formalized. This place is paid for. We will sell the condo. I thought we would just live here and create a sustainable permaculture estate and eventually do some tours and workshops and show the world what off-grid living could be like. What you think? The neighboring cottage is for sale so we could use it for the meetings and workshops and also plant more fruit trees over there. It's another one and a half acres." Jenna embraced him. "Really, oh, Étienne. Really? What a dream!" Étienne cupped her face. "We'll be homesteaders with money, cherie." Jenna smiled, "And can we have hens for eggs?"

"Yes," said Étienne hugging her. "We can have up to five hens in Barrie but we're not zoned for larger livestock so just chickens, veggies and fruit. Any meat we'll have to order."

Jenna hugged him tightly against her. She could feel butterflies in her stomach she was so happy. She and Philippe saw him off telling him they would have a roast chicken ready on his return at seven.

Jenna and Philippe took the dogs out and then got ready for the drive to the doctor's. They had an appointment just north of the 400 at a new clinic. It was a 20 minute drive but the doctors came well-recommended and Étienne had been able to get them taken on as patients which was no easy feat with the Doctor shortage. And it was good they had their appointment that day. Environment Canada had posted the storm warning for the next day. Winter planned one last hurrah.

They were early setting out so Jenna decided to get the groceries on the way. She looked proudly at her new car as she and Philippe stowed the bags in the trunk. The car was a real beauty but was hardly visible under the snow that covered it. Jenna looked around. Huge snowflakes fell furiously as she brushed off the car. She thought briefly of cancelling the appointment but didn't think the snow could last long. The blizzard wasn't expected until the next day. It was probably just a pre-storm flurry.

At the first stoplight she looked back at Philippe sleeping in his car seat. The wind was picking up and the snow fell thickly. She drove onwards carefully, aware of the responsibility of her precious cargo. As she came up the ramp onto the highway, she saw that other cars were slowing and having trouble keeping to their lanes. The snow was so heavy that the white divisions between the lanes were invisible. Her headlights pierced only a few feet ahead.

Jenna flipped on the all-news station and a weather update was on. Strong winds had moved the storm rapidly and it had now hit southern Ontario with a great force. It was heading north.

The 401 was closed in numerous places due to white-out conditions and a 67 car pileup. The 400 was not mentioned but Jenna, her hands white knuckled on the steering wheel wished the 400 had closed before she got on it. She could not see. She had never driven in such conditions before even though she had spent most of her life in the Snowbelt.

Jenna eased the car as far onto the shoulder as she dared, turned on her four-way flashers, and reached for her new cell phone. She called Étienne. He told her that she should stay put, run the car periodically to keep warm, but make sure that the tailpipe was not blocked by snow so that there was no risk of carbon monoxide poisoning. Jenna called and cancelled their appointments. The receptionist said that everyone was cancelling and they were closing early.

Very few cars were passing and Jenna could see at least 4 inches of new snow on the hood. An hour passed and Philippe woke up needing to pee. After he finished, Jenna tried to brush all the snow off of him before popping him into the front seat beside her. She wished the police would come and rescue them. But when she had called 911 they had said she just had to sit tight as there were numerous accidents and stranded cars. The radio announced that the police were closing the 400 both ways between Barrie and Parry Sound. Did that mean Étienne would not be able to get to them?

Philippe played beside her eating the snacks from the grocery bags. She had brought all the non-frozen stuff into the car. In the trunk, she had found an emergency kit and a sleeping bag. Étienne had ordered everything for the car. She was thankful. He was the most resourceful person she knew. She opened up the sleeping bag and tucked it around Philippe's legs. The emergency pack contained a fleece blanket, mitts and scarf, a knit hat and socks, 2 hand warmers and 2 foot warmers, candles, matches, a flashlight, batteries, and a foldout shovel. She bundled them both up more and set one of the candles in the tin provided on the dashboard. Its cheery light made them smile.

Étienne called every 30 minutes which gave Jenna some comfort but she finally faced the fact that she and Philippe might be spending the night in the car. She worried about the dogs but Étienne might be able to make it that far.

She and Philippe ate sandwiches made of the cold cuts and cheeses they had bought. Jenna thought about trying to locate someone in another car but remembered learning it was always best to stay with the car. She used the shovel to dig out around the exhaust as the car was now half covered in snow. Philippe thankfully fell asleep after a cranky hour. It was his bedtime now. Jenna sat with her hands on her tummy and suddenly her whole world quaked and realigned.

She had felt the baby move. She had felt the baby move inside her. Pieces fell into place. She hadn't had her period. It had just been spotting. She hadn't missed her period the next month due to the misadventure. She had been pregnant. She felt it again, unmistakable, like a butterfly moving along her lower belly. She wanted to cry with joy. Why, she must be at least four months' pregnant. She, Jenna, was going to have a baby! She felt her breasts. They were so full and eager. She felt her gently rounded tummy. She did her coat back up hugging her body to herself.

Jenna picked up her cell phone and called Étienne. "Étienne, did you know? I didn't know. I can't believe it. I have just realized we are going to have a baby. The baby was kicking!" There was a silence on the other end for a moment. Jenna held her breath until Étienne responded. "You didn't know? I was so worried. I thought you didn't want the baby or weren't sure about staying with me. The doctor told me in North Bay and I was waiting for you to talk to me. Are you happy?" Jenna smiled into the darkness, "I am. I am. I have dreamt of having a baby. I can't believe it!" Étienne sighed, "Are you warm enough? How is Philippe?" Jenna answered, "He's here in the sleeping bag asleep. I had better go check the exhaust is clear and then I'll turn the car on again. I'm going to move into the back seat so I can wrap the bag around me too. My feet are starting to send signals. Not too happy."

Étienne cleared his throat, "The police wouldn't let me continue on the 400. I had to exit and am now almost home. I'll let the dogs out and think what to do. Wait for me."

After struggling to shovel out the area behind the exhaust, Jenna climbed into the front and turned the car on brushing as much snow off herself as she could and then climbing into the back where she wriggled into the sleeping bag with Philippe. She was shivering. The car read minus 18°C. It had to be a record for mid-April. Jenna started to get worried, but the car soon warmed up again. She nibbled on some biscuits and hoped to sleep, but sleep eluded her. After 30 minutes, Jenna switched the car off again. It seemed pretty good on gas for the tank was still at the halfway mark now. Étienne called again. "Ma chere femme. Tell me how many kilometers are on the car now? Okay, you are probably about 12 kilometers from the on ramp. Hold tight."

As she lay in the dark, a memory came to Jenna. Mrs. G had a new foster child. Mikey was a boy about 10 years old. They had taken the kids to the quarry to spend that first afternoon. The boy had been so thin. His lips had turned blue and he had been shivering and shaking and he and Jenna sat together on a rock in the warm sun. The bruises on his young body weren't even starting to heal yet. Jenna realized that she had a lot to be thankful for. She had had loving parents even though they had died too soon. That night she had already heard Mrs. G changing the sheets once and worried about Mrs. G's arthritis, Jenna had gotten up to help with changing the bed.

Jenna took Mikey for a quick shower and passed him clean pajamas from their stock. When they came back to the bedroom the bed was stripped. Mikey said "Now you hate me right? I'm nothing but trouble. Nobody wanted me anyway." His voice trembled with stress but Mrs. G. looked at him sternly and replied, "I don't pay no never mind to other people's opinions. You wouldn't be here if I didn't want you. I should have shown you before. Look at this bed. I cover the mattress with one of my washable waterproof fabric shower curtains. I got a pile at the second-hand store. Know what else I got there? Come Jenna. Open the linen closet." In the closet were sheets piled in color sections. From the character pile, Mrs. G pulled out Power Rangers, Avengers, and Superman.

"Look at all these sheets. Someone gave them to the charity store so we could get them. Why you can have accidents all night and we'll have no problem. What will you have next?" Mikey's thin arm reached out for Hulk Hogan sheets and then he chose the Marvel blanket. He was shivering again so they quickly made up his bed. Mrs. G. reminded him to just ring the little school bell again if he needed them, tousled his hair, and turned off the light. With a kind word of thanks and a nod at Jenna, she headed back to her room but then she paused and looked at Jenna saying, "Love is planning and hard work. You remember that my girl."

Now Jenna sat wrapped in the sleeping bag in the cold car. Why had she just been waiting? How had she forgotten to act? When they were rescued, she would get down to some hard work. She planned what she needed to say. She would work hard to make Mrs. G. proud of her and her growing family.

Sometime later Jenna heard a tapping on the passenger window. Philippe started to cry as he woke up. Jenna held her cell phone in her hand and lowered the back window suddenly afraid. Étienne's face loomed through the opening. "We are here to the rescue. Hey buddy, how would you like to ride on a snowmobile back to town?" Jenna shut the window, reached forward and turned off the car, and unlocked the door. "Come out of that bag you two." Étienne pulled Philippe out, held him, and bustled Jenna onto the back of the skidoo behind a muffled driver. Philippe sat on Étienne's lap behind another driver and all three were fastened into helmets. They left the car and headed slowly through the thickly falling snow.

Jenna clung to her driver and closed her eyes. She couldn't imagine how they were finding their way on the hilly terrain that skirted the highway. After what seemed like a long time, they stopped. They were in front of Étienne's car in a parking lot on the edge of town. Jenna was helped into the passenger seat and Philippe was buckled into his car seat in the back. Étienne shook hands and clapped the snowsuit man on the back and got in, driving carefully home. "Nisha put me in touch with these guys. A Mohawk warrior's what you want when the going is tough. I've invited them to a feast on Sunday to give thanks." Jenna smiled. She was so grateful not to have had to spend the night in the car. She rested her hand on her belly and Étienne's covered hers. "Let's get my family home." he said driving steadily through the storm.

Jenna was so glad to be back in their cosy cottage. The great room was warm and Étienne soon had a roaring fire adding more warmth and comfort. She and Philippe had baths while Étienne heated some soup and made toasted cheese and tomato sandwiches.

Philippe went to bed quite willingly and Jenna returned to sit across from Étienne. "Loving is hard work." she reminded herself. She took his hands and told him all about her upset and confusion over Clarisse and her unbelievable failure to recognize her pregnancy. She described how happy she was to be with him and expecting a baby and how much she loved him and Philippe.

Étienne rose, sat beside her, and lifted her into his arms and rocked her. "I've loved you since that first day in the copying room. When we sat over French onion soup and you revealed how sweet and gentle and caring and interesting and funny and sensitive you were, I felt that I had found my soul mate. We were two lonely people who needed each other. We had both lost badly at a relationship but your wounds were fresh. I needed to give you time. But I wanted to be with you. I wanted to look after you. I was so happy in Montréal. Argentina was wonderful because we were together. I was so happy to get you and Philippe in one fell swoop when we married." Jenna watched the firelight flicker across his beloved face, "But Clarisse. You seemed to want Clarisse too."

"Mon amore. Clarisse's life has not been easy. She is now at a retreat up north called Grail Springs and I'm paying for it. I was worried about her state of mind at that time and what she might do. Can you understand that I loved her once and still care for her? She suffered terrible abuse once and she doesn't know how to love. She doesn't even know how to love herself."

Jenna blinked and swallowed. "I'm sorry and you had a child together. Of course you felt some responsibility."

"Jenna, Clarisse and I have a child together but he is not my biological son. She came back to me pregnant and I was glad. I thought the baby might settle her and I gladly accepted the child. Clarisse is going to let us legally adopt Philippe. She'll surrender her rights so we know he's safe with us but I want them to know each other."

"Now, let me tell you how much I love you." And with that Étienne began kissing Jenna most satisfactorily. Moments later she smiled, "Actually, you haven't said a word." Étienne laughed, "Oh yes, I did say I was going to tell you how much I love you but let me show you instead. My dear baby mama. Let's make love." Lying in Étienne's arms with her hand against her belly, Jenna knew that this was her spring. She smiled into his eyes and he said, "I love you." just as she felt the baby move. "I love you too." she replied. She fell asleep dreaming of babies and gardens.

When she awoke Étienne and Philippe were setting up a tray to serve her breakfast in bed. Jim stood wagging his tail and Zoey was prancing around the bed. "Do we need a bigger house Jenna?" Étienne asked. "Not at all." Jenna replied. "We have everything we need here. Mrs. G would be so happy for me. Can we plant a huge field of sunflowers for her?" Étienne replied, "We can."

And they did. That spring, Philippe scattered seeds in a wide arch around their garden. In September, Jenna sat, baby suckling at her breast, watching father and son harvest the seeds from the great drooping heads of sunflowers. Winter was coming but spring would follow once again.

Printed in Great Britain
by Amazon

83259701R00078